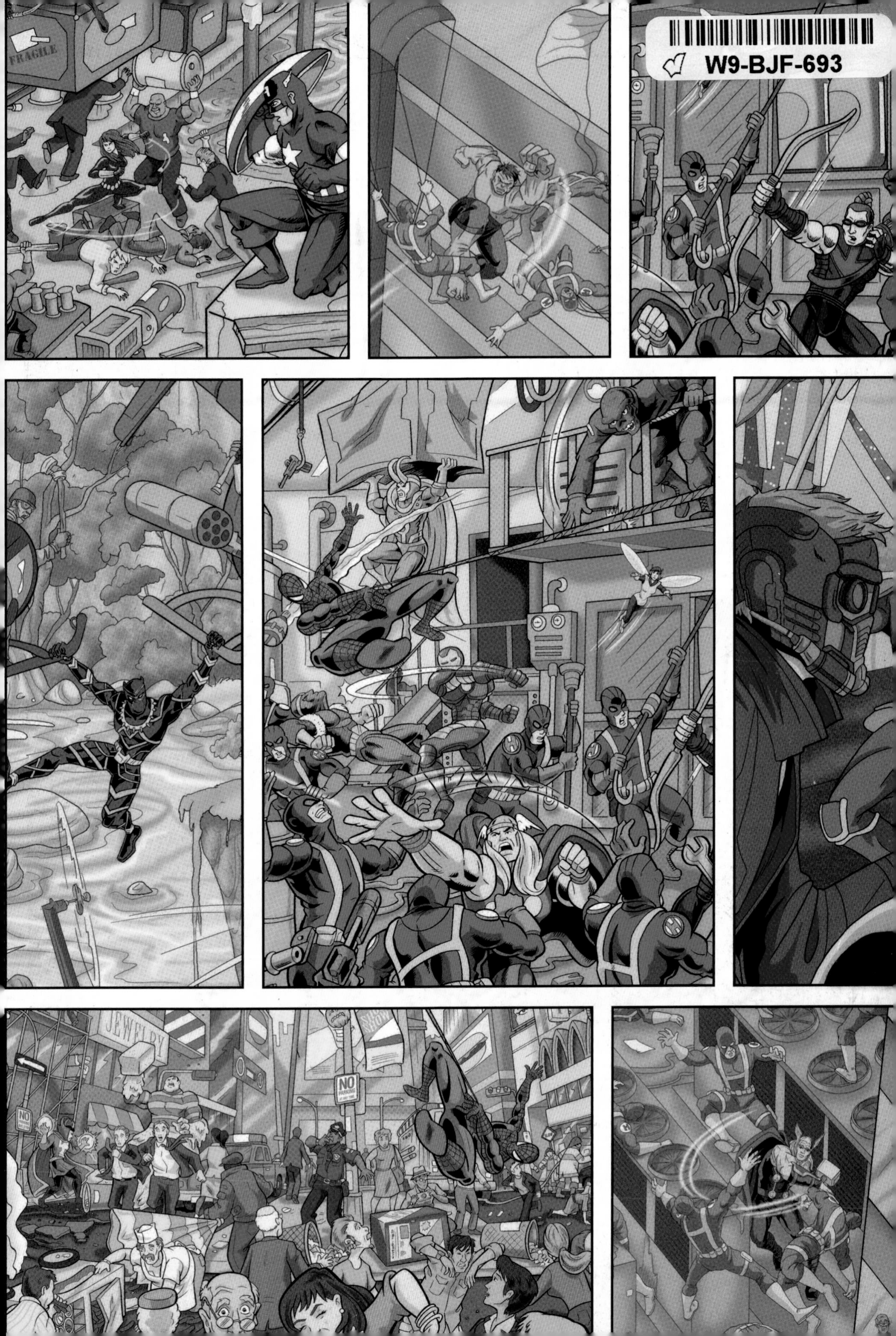
FRAGILE
JEWELRY
NO PARKING

Illustrated by Art Mawhinney

Published by PI Kids, an imprint of Phoenix International Publications, Inc.

8501 West Higgins Road   34 Seymour Street   Heimhuder Straße 81
Chicago, Illinois 60631   London W1H 7JE   20148 Hamburg

PI Kids is a trademark of
Phoenix International Publications, Inc., and is registered in the United States.

Look and Find is a trademark of Phoenix International Publications, Inc., and is
registered in the United States, Canada, and the United Kingdom.

Customer Service: 1-877-277-9441
or customerservice@pikidsmedia.com
www.pikidsmedia.com

ISBN: 978-1-5037-4789-0

BEST OF MARVEL

pi kids ®

An imprint of Phoenix International Publications, Inc.

Chicago • London • New York • Hamburg • Mexico City • Sydney

Look and Find ®

With comics and films going back for decades, Marvel is a fixture in popular culture—and for good reason. Iconic characters like Spider-Man and Black Panther delight and inspire us, bringing humor, heart, and heroics in their quest to make the world a better place.

Now, these heroes need your help. Look for your favorite good guys in this book's scenes, which capture exciting moments from across the Marvel Universe. But watch out: there are villains lurking in the shadows!

Meet the Heroes...

The Avengers

Captain America is the leader of the Avengers and a hero out of time. The Super-Soldier Serum that gave him his powers also helped him survive, frozen in ice, for decades. Look for him, and his iconic red, white, and blue shield, as he continues to fight evil in the modern day.

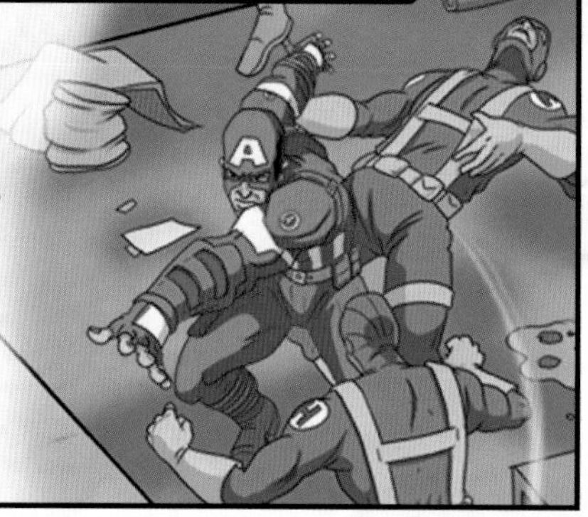

Colonel Nick Fury is the Director of S.H.I.E.L.D., which means he probably knows more about you than you do. Although he normally works behind the scenes, keep an eye out for him displaying his mastery of hand-to-hand combat and military strategy.

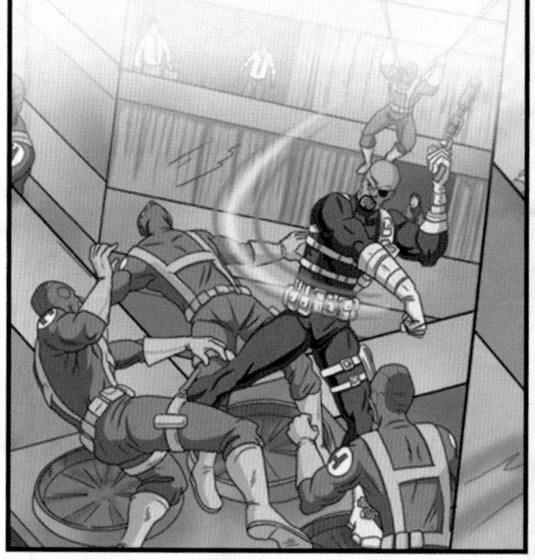

Thor is a hero of myth, and heir to the throne of Asgard. Strong, fast, and virtually immortal, Thor can usually be found in the thick of the action. Look for him wielding his legendary hammer Mjolnir.

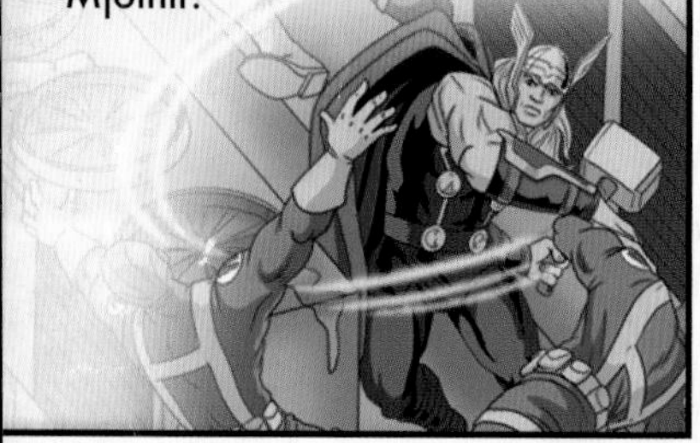

Bruce Banner when calm, **Hulk** when enraged, this hero can smash any evil in his path. With his size and strength, he's not hard to spot—find him wherever the Avengers need his help.

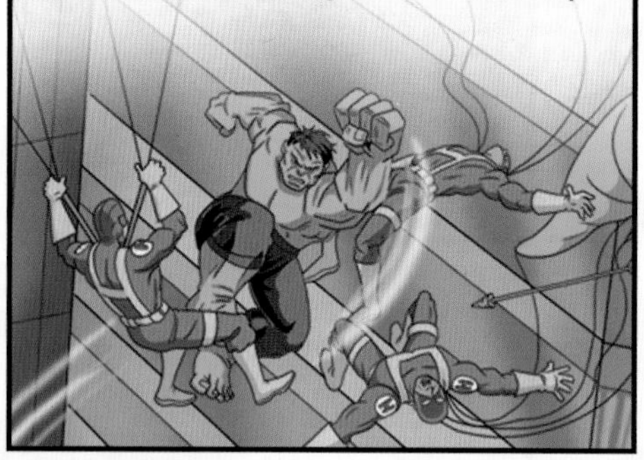

Iron Man fights crime all over the globe, but his home is Stark Industries, where he's always at the cutting edge of engineering, using his resources and intellect to protect the world. Look for him flying the red and gold armor he built himself.

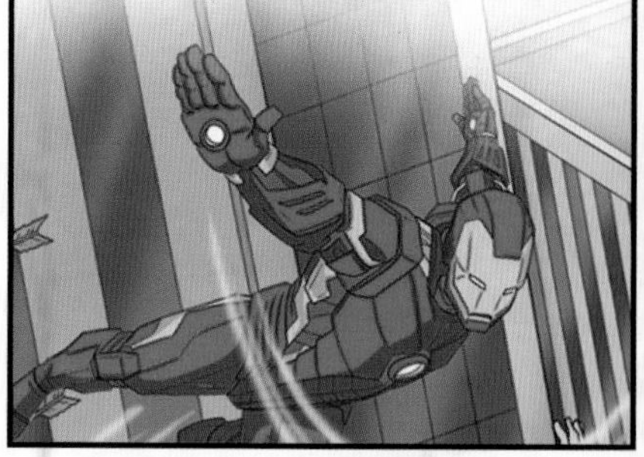

Black Widow may not have superhuman powers, but don't underestimate her—she's a master of combat and espionage. Look for her using stun batons, martial arts, or anything within reach as she fights to protect the innocent.

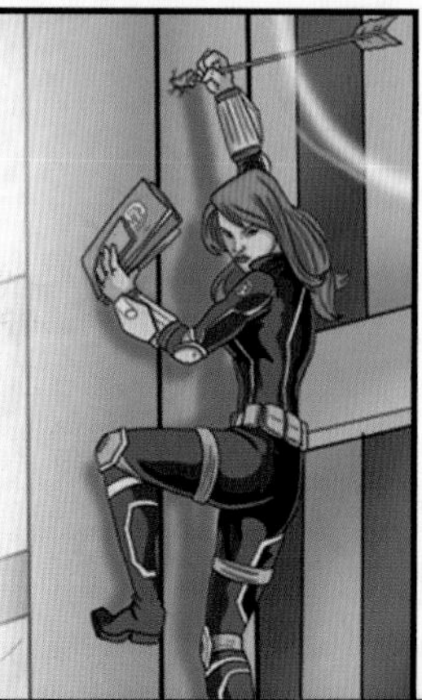

Ant-Man and **Wasp** are super heroes at any size—and they can be many different sizes! Just as strong when they're tiny, these heroes regularly team up to save the day. Can you find them whatever their size?

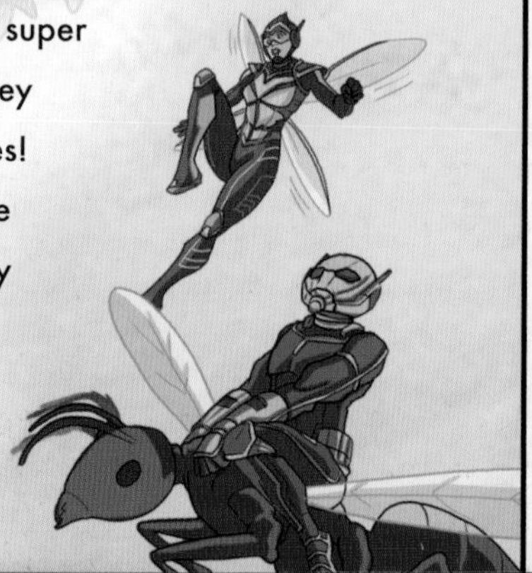

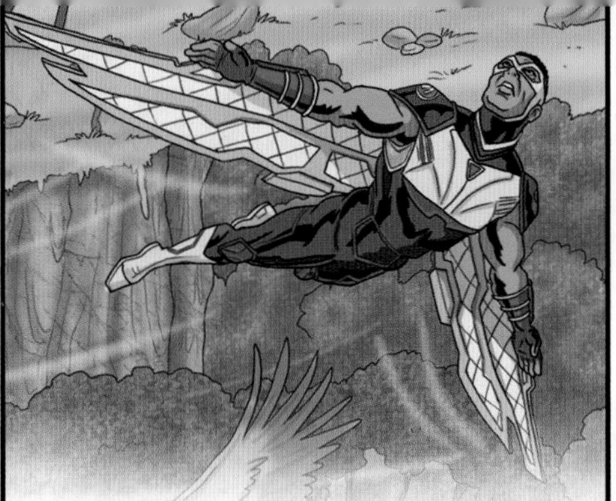

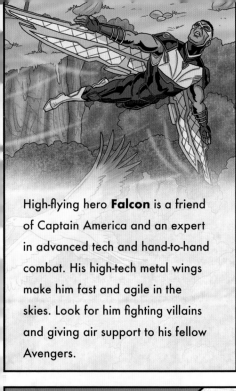

High-flying hero **Falcon** is a friend of Captain America and an expert in advanced tech and hand-to-hand combat. His high-tech metal wings make him fast and agile in the skies. Look for him fighting villains and giving air support to his fellow Avengers.

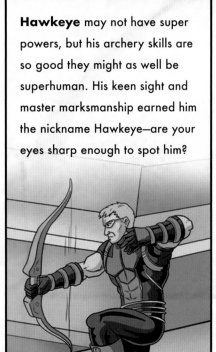

Hawkeye may not have super powers, but his archery skills are so good they might as well be superhuman. His keen sight and master marksmanship earned him the nickname Hawkeye—are your eyes sharp enough to spot him?

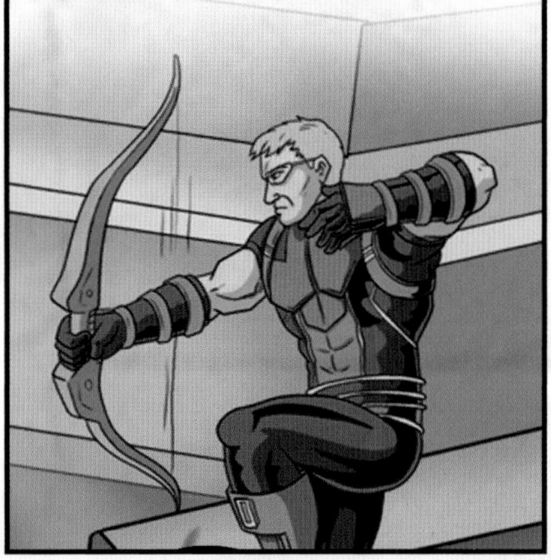

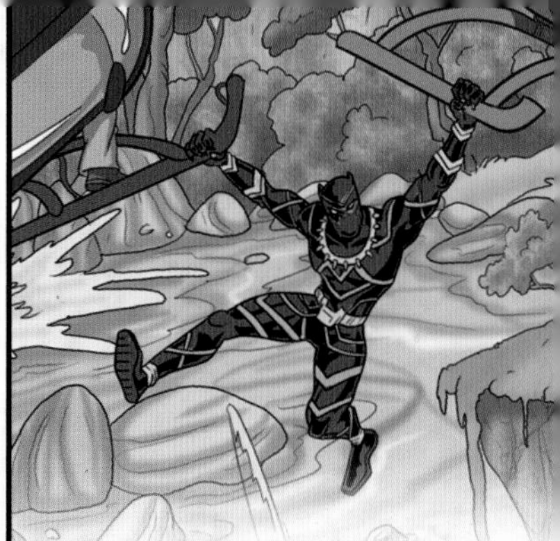

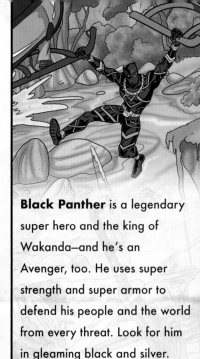

Black Panther is a legendary super hero and the king of Wakanda—and he's an Avenger, too. He uses super strength and super armor to defend his people and the world from every threat. Look for him in gleaming black and silver.

Spider-Man

Spider-Man is a wall-crawling, web-slinging super hero—and science nerd—with a special sense for danger. When he's not stuck in high school, you can find him up in the air and down on the ground, protecting the citizens of New York.

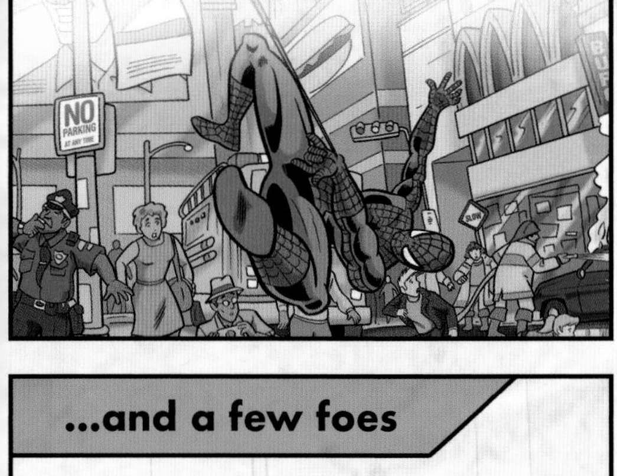
NO
PARKING

The Guardians of the Galaxy

The Guardians of the Galaxy are a rough-and-tumble crew of outlaw heroes from across the galaxy. Led by Star-Lord, this crew is as likely to get into mischief as save the day, but when the chips are down, these heroes always come through. Whether helping the Avengers on Earth or defeating villains in outer space, look for this ragtag bunch fighting evil in their own way.

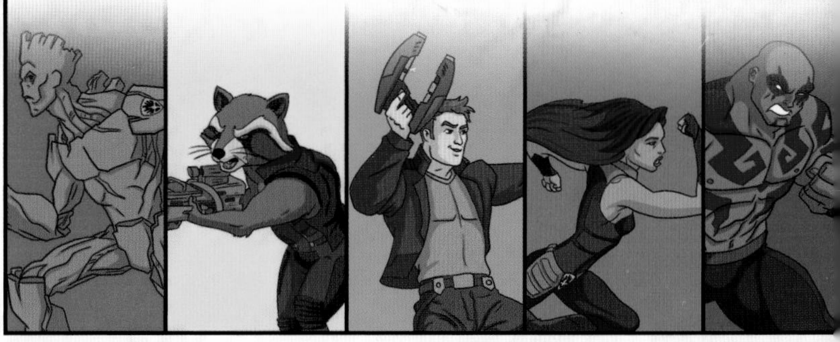

...and a few foes

Thanos is a powerful tyrant with incredible strength and armies at his command. Whether out in space or here on Earth, Guardians and Avengers alike have fought hard to protect the universe from his crimes. Look for him wreaking havoc in his quest for power.

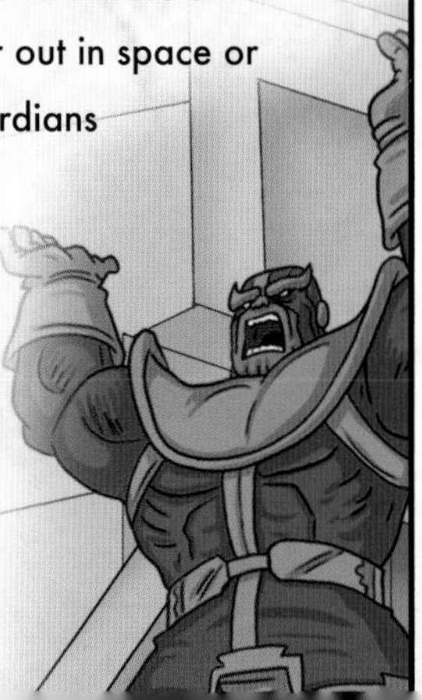

Thor's brother **Loki** is as sneaky and ruthless as Thor is loyal and heroic. Loki is a master of manipulation and illusions, so keep a wary eye out for this shapeshifter.

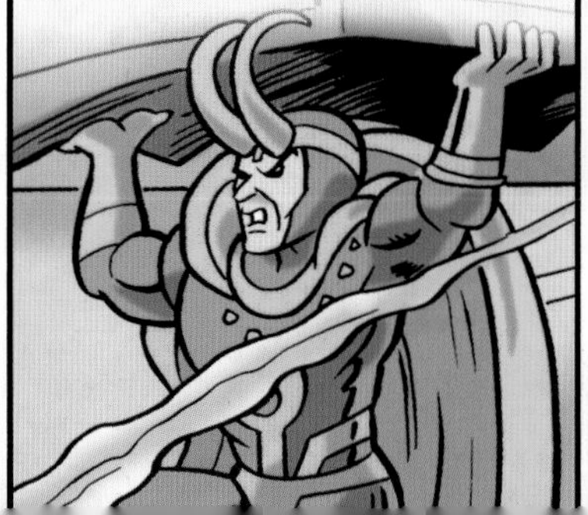

Red Skull's strength comes from the same serum that transformed Captain America... but in Red Skull's case, the process also gave him his menacing skull-like appearance. Be on the lookout for this villain and his army of deadly Hydra soldiers.

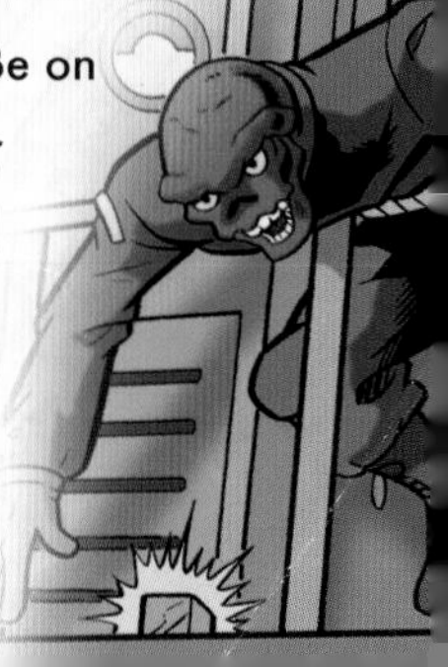

THE AVENGERS ARE IN A BIND! HYDRA'S AGENTS HAVE AMBUSHED A SECRET MEETING HIGH ABOVE THE CITY STREETS. NOW BLACK WIDOW MUST MAKE A QUICK GETAWAY BEFORE HYDRA CAN STEAL S.H.I.E.L.D.'S LATEST MISSION PLANS.

WHILE HAWKEYE LENDS A HELPING HAND, SPOT THESE OCCUPIED AVENGERS...AND LOOK OUT FOR INNOCENT BYSTANDERS!

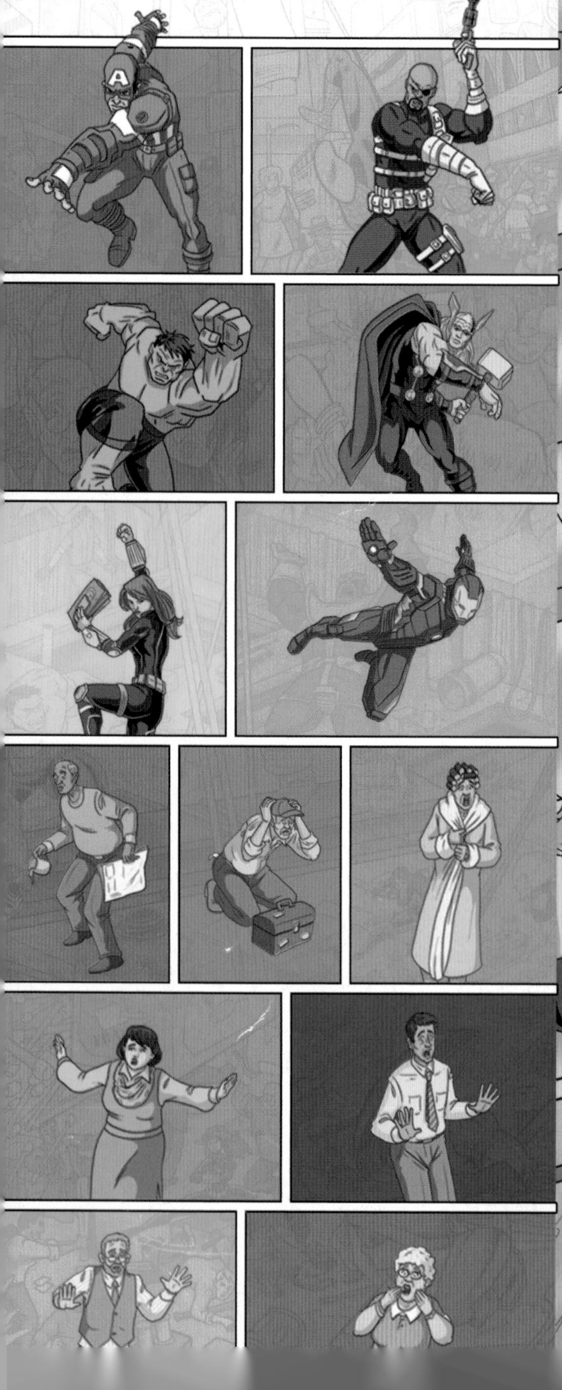

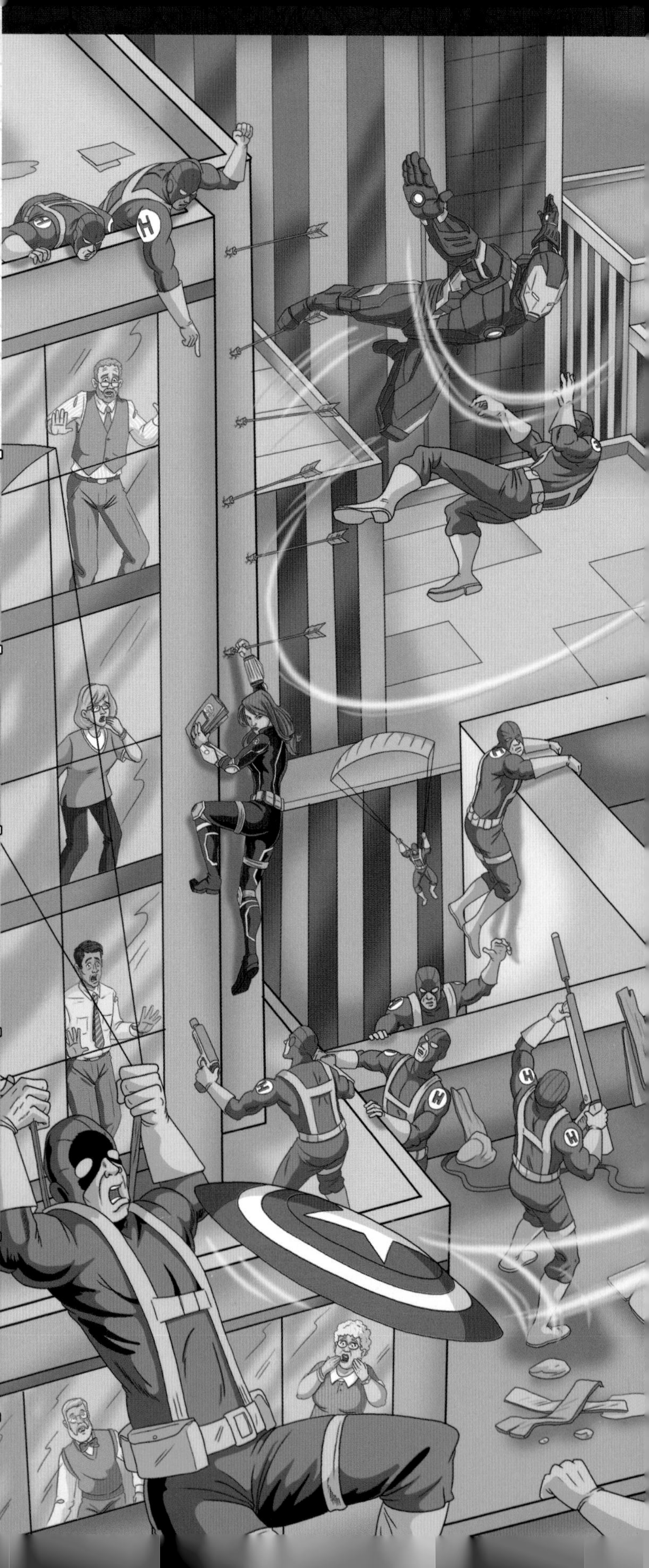

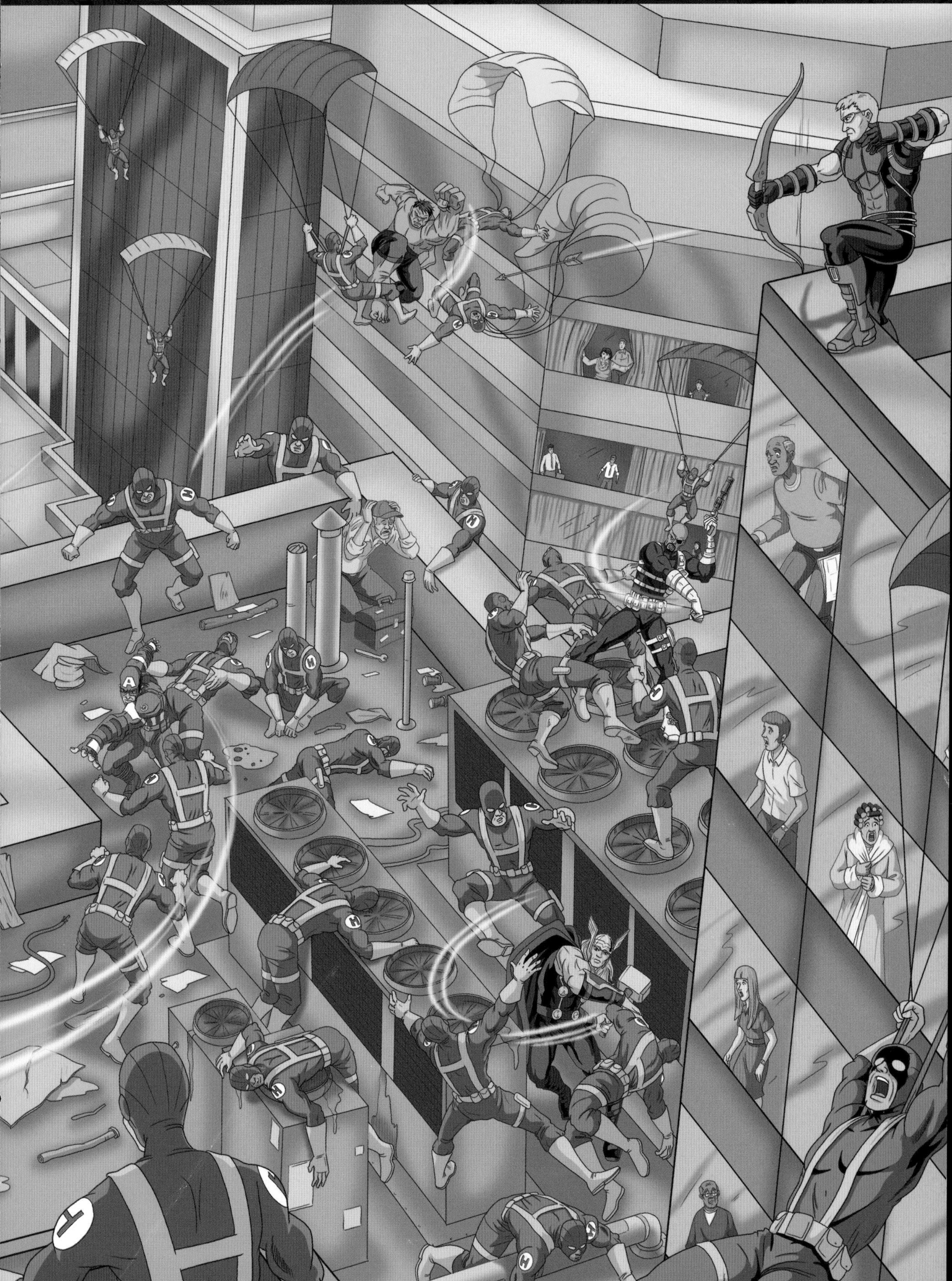

XANDAR IS UNDER ATTACK! THE GUARDIANS OF THE GALAXY ARRIVE TO SAVE THE PLANET AND ITS PEOPLE FROM RONAN'S EVILS.

AS STAR-LORD AND FRIENDS BATTLE RONAN'S ARMY, HELP THEM KEEP AN EYE OUT FOR THESE SOARING SPACESHIPS AND ADVERSARIAL ALIENS:

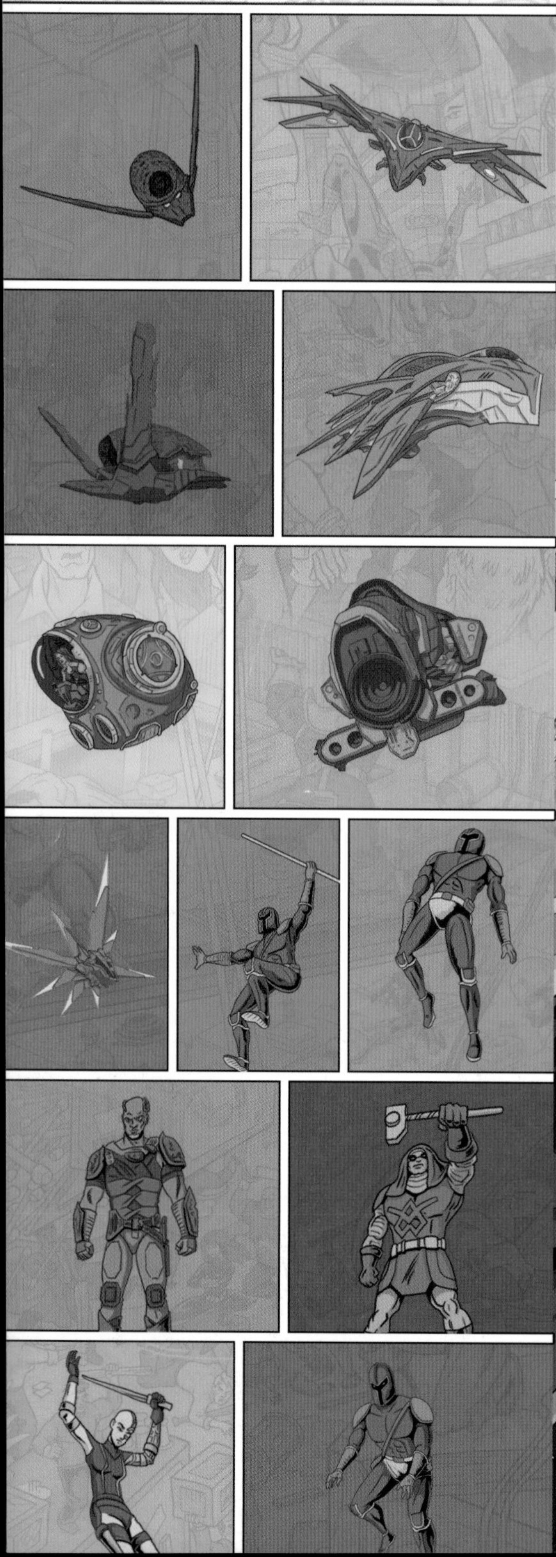

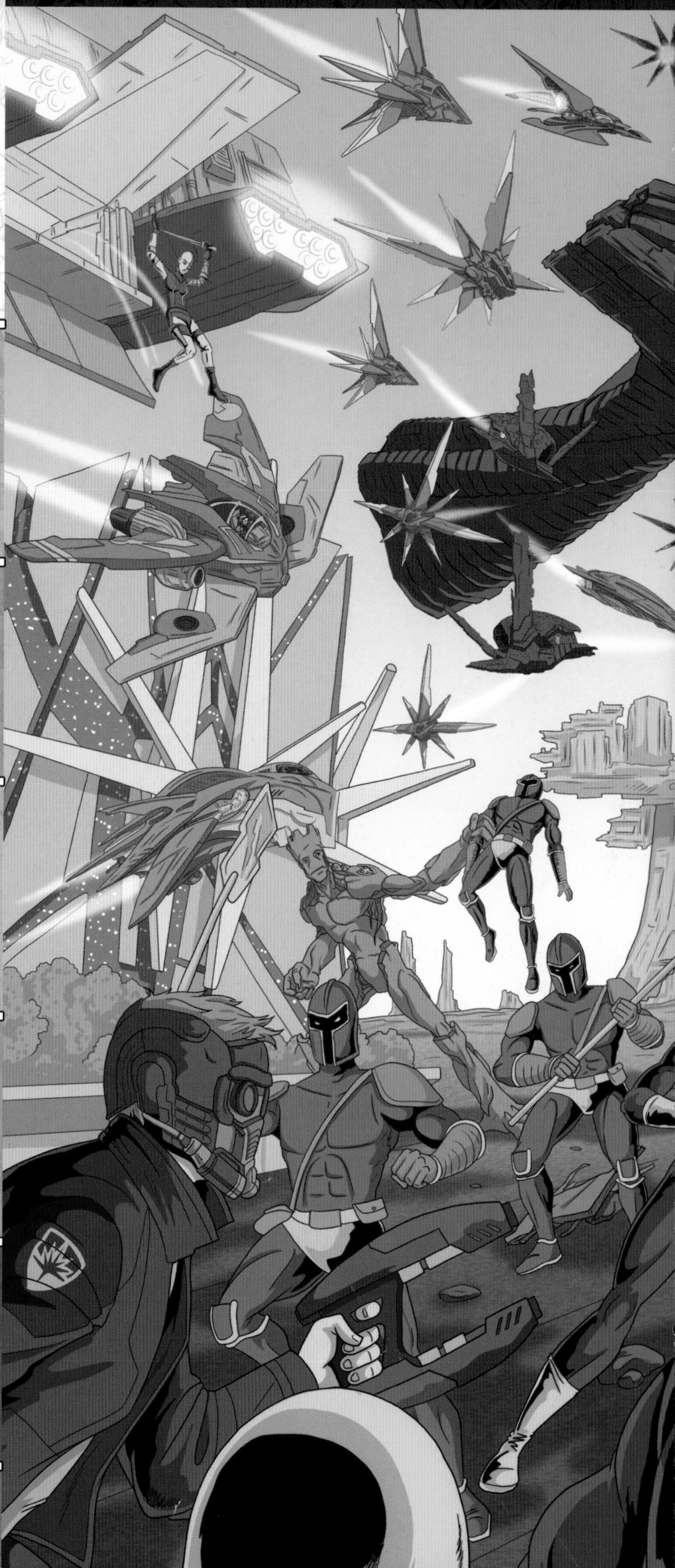

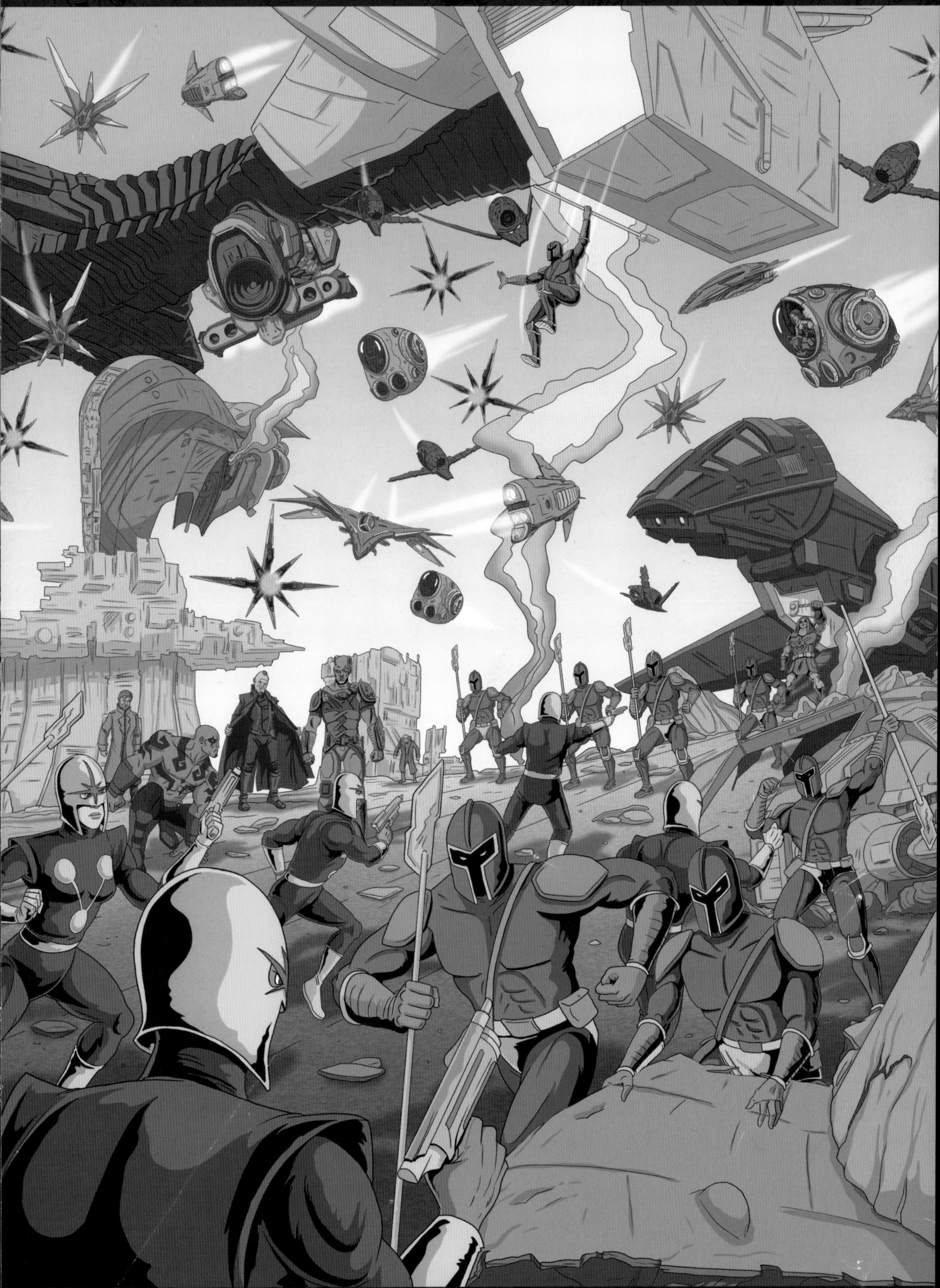

THANOS HAS COME TO EARTH, AND HE'S LOOKING FOR THE INFINITY GEMS. IF HE GETS HIS HANDS ON THE GEMS, HE WILL HAVE MORE POWER THAN ANYONE CAN POSSIBLY IMAGINE.

HELP THE AVENGERS LOCATE THE INFINITY GEMS BEFORE THANOS DOES! AND WHILE THEY'RE FIGHTING, SEE IF YOU CAN SPOT THESE OBJECTS THE AVENGERS COULD USE FOR COVER:

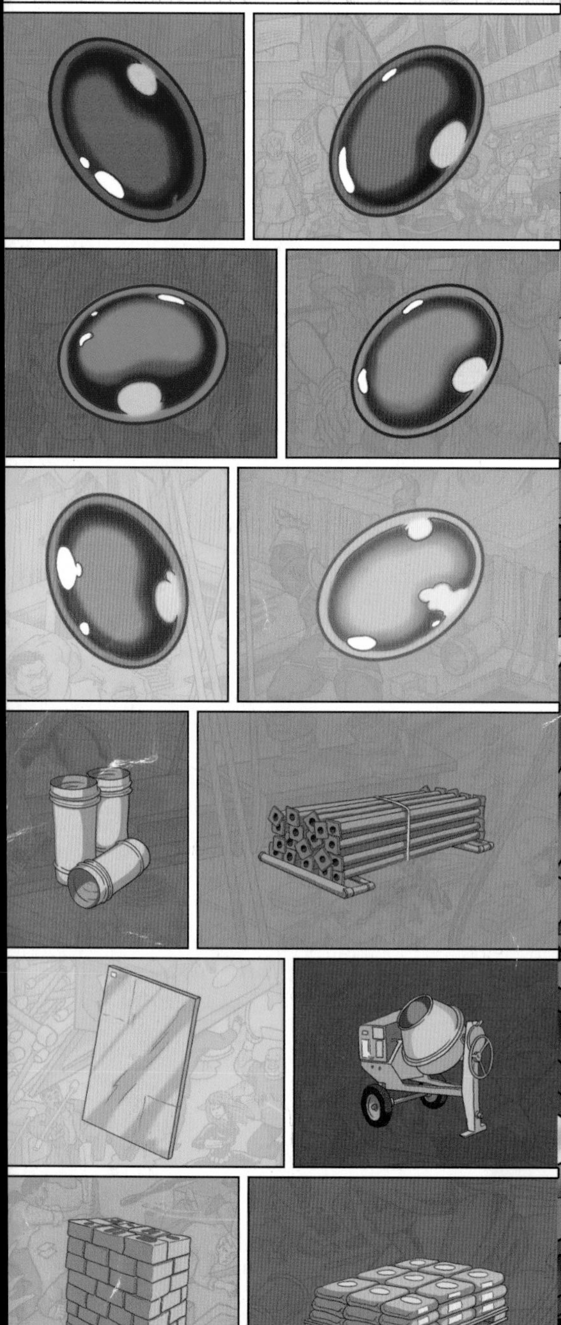

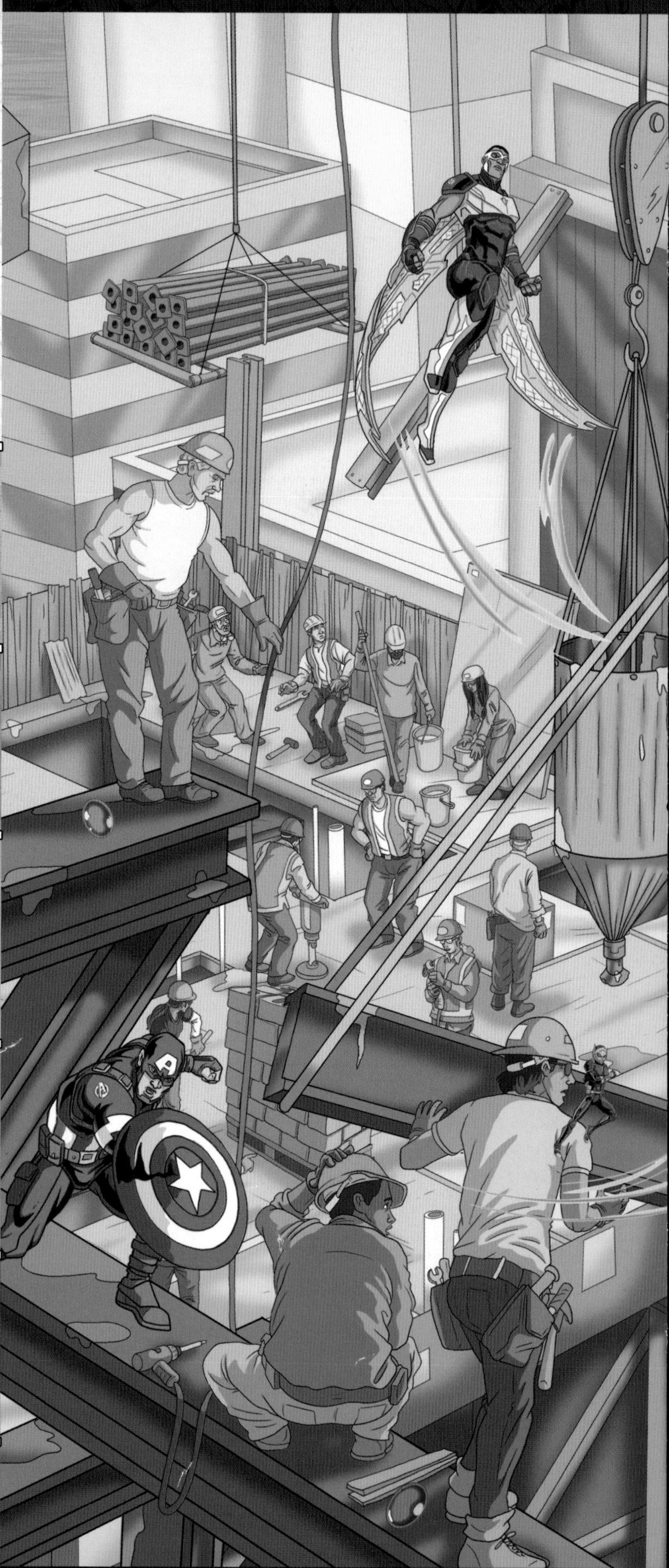

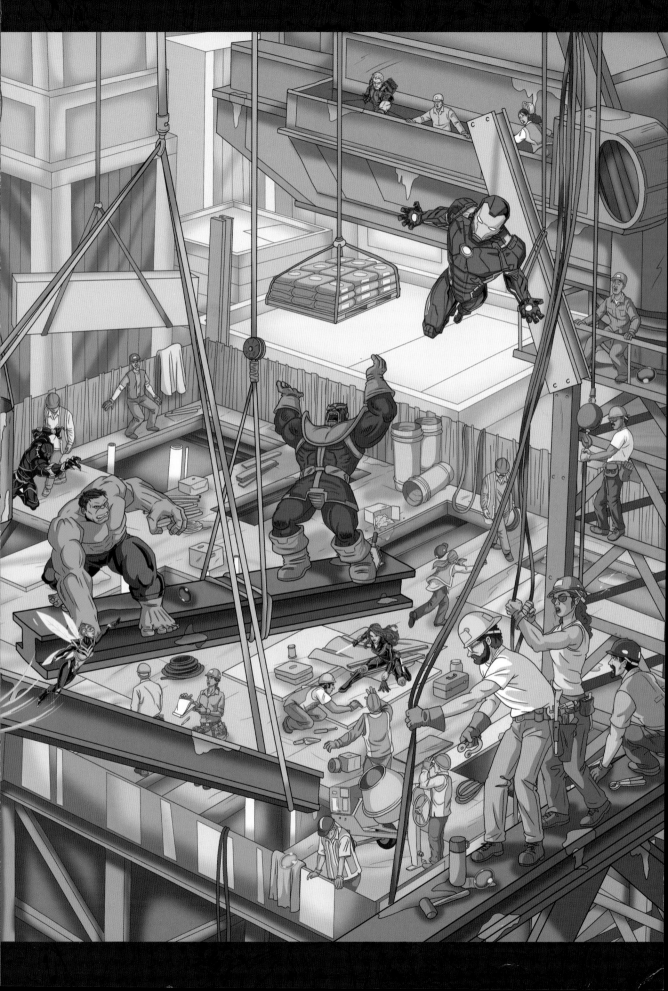

JUST WHEN THE AVENGERS FINALLY GET A DAY OFF, SANDMAN AND GREEN GOBLIN HAVE TEAMED UP TO TAKE OVER THE AMUSEMENT PARK! BUT SPIDER-MAN IS IN TOWN AS WELL, AND HE DOESN'T FIND THIS DUO SO AMUSING.

AS OUR HEROES BATTLE TWO FOR THE PRICE OF ONE, SEARCH FOR THESE THINGS THEY WOULD RATHER BE ENJOYING, INCLUDING 20 TUFTS OF COTTON CANDY—WHICH MIGHT EVEN BE ENOUGH FOR HULK!

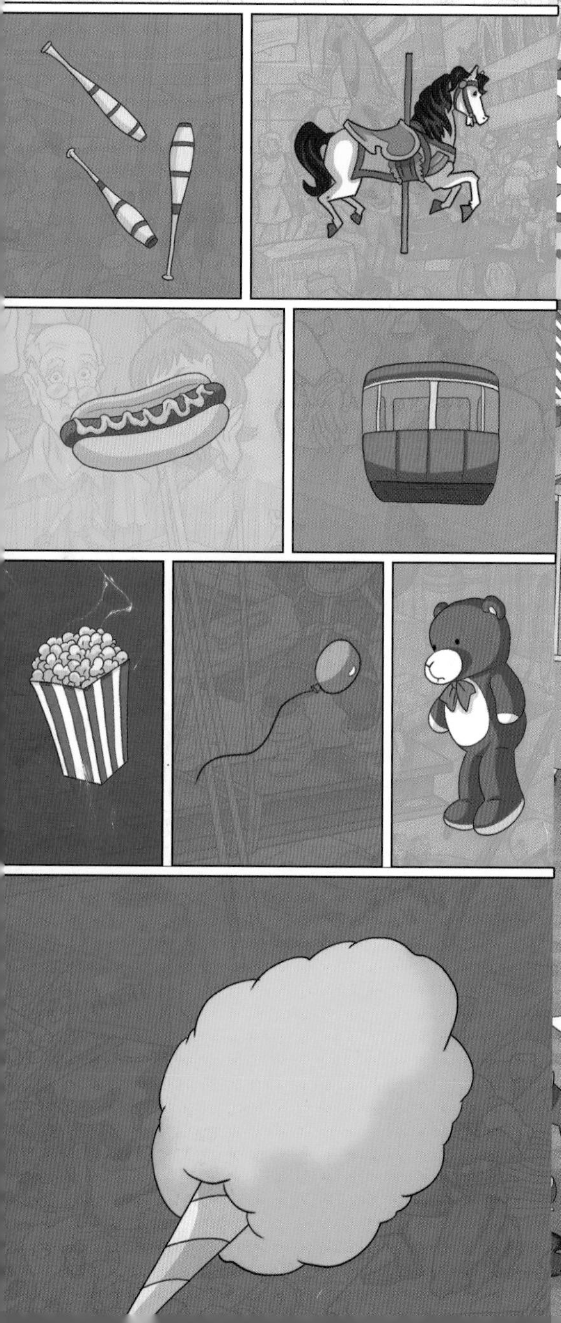

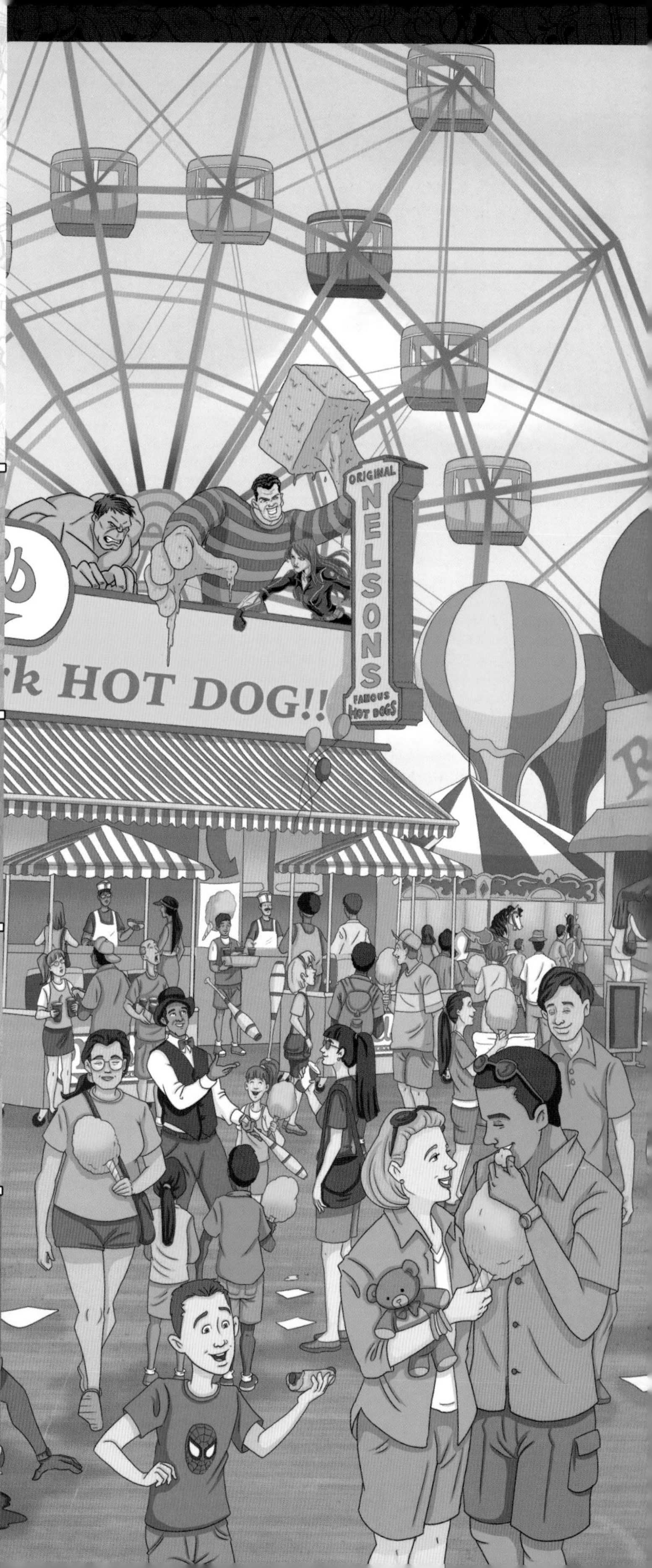
ORIGINAL NELSONS FAMOUS HOT DOGS
HOT DOG!!

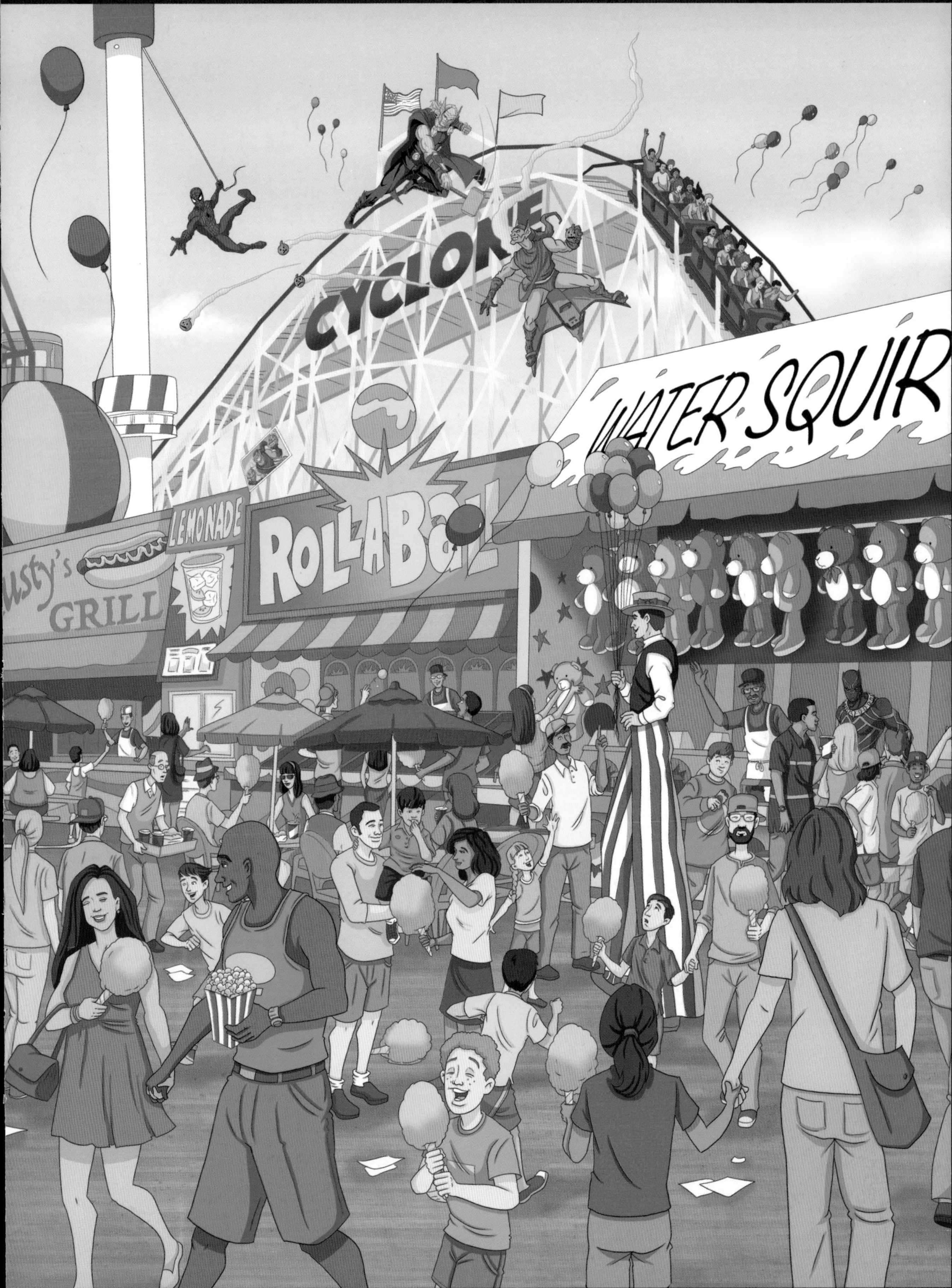
CYCLONE
WATER SQUIR
LEMONADE
ROLL-A-BALL
usty's
GRILL

IRON MAN HAS FLOWN TO THE FROZEN EDGE OF THE ARCTIC CIRCLE. IN THIS LAND OF ICE AND SNOW, TITANIUM MAN AND AN ARMY OF VILLAINS ARE PLOTTING TO DESTROY THE EARTH.

AS IRON MAN STOPS THEM FROM BLOWING UP THE WORLD, HELP HIM AVOID RADIATION—AND COLLISIONS—BY FINDING THESE RADIOACTIVE ITEMS AND THINGS THAT FLY:

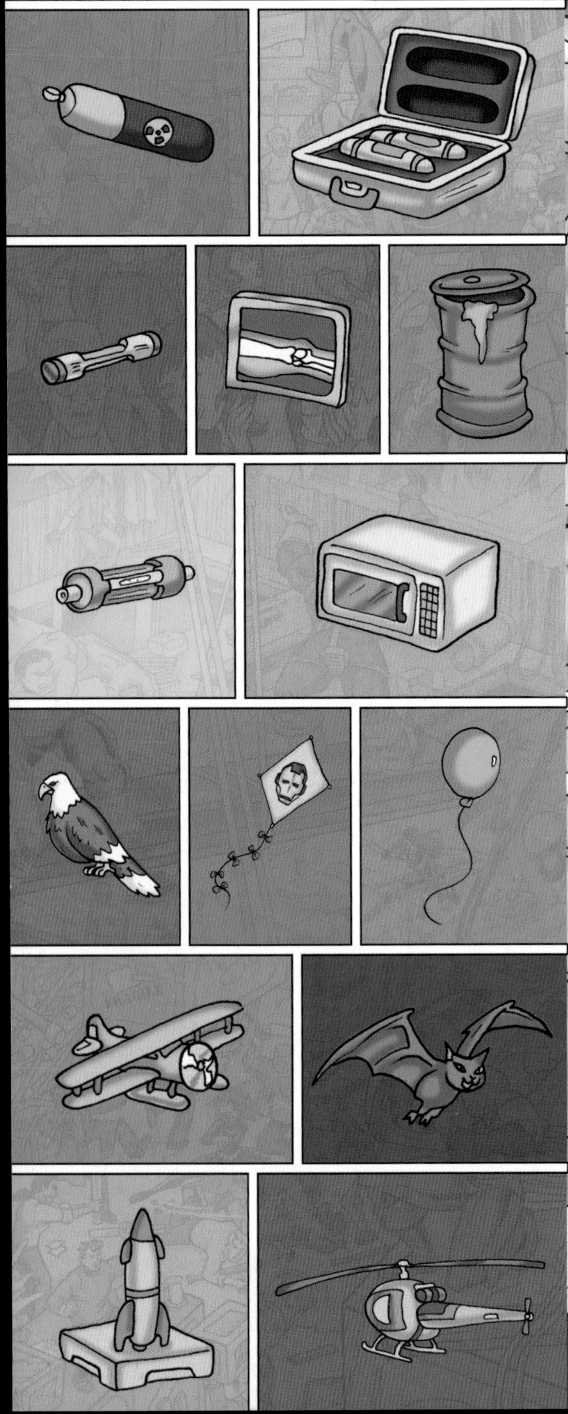

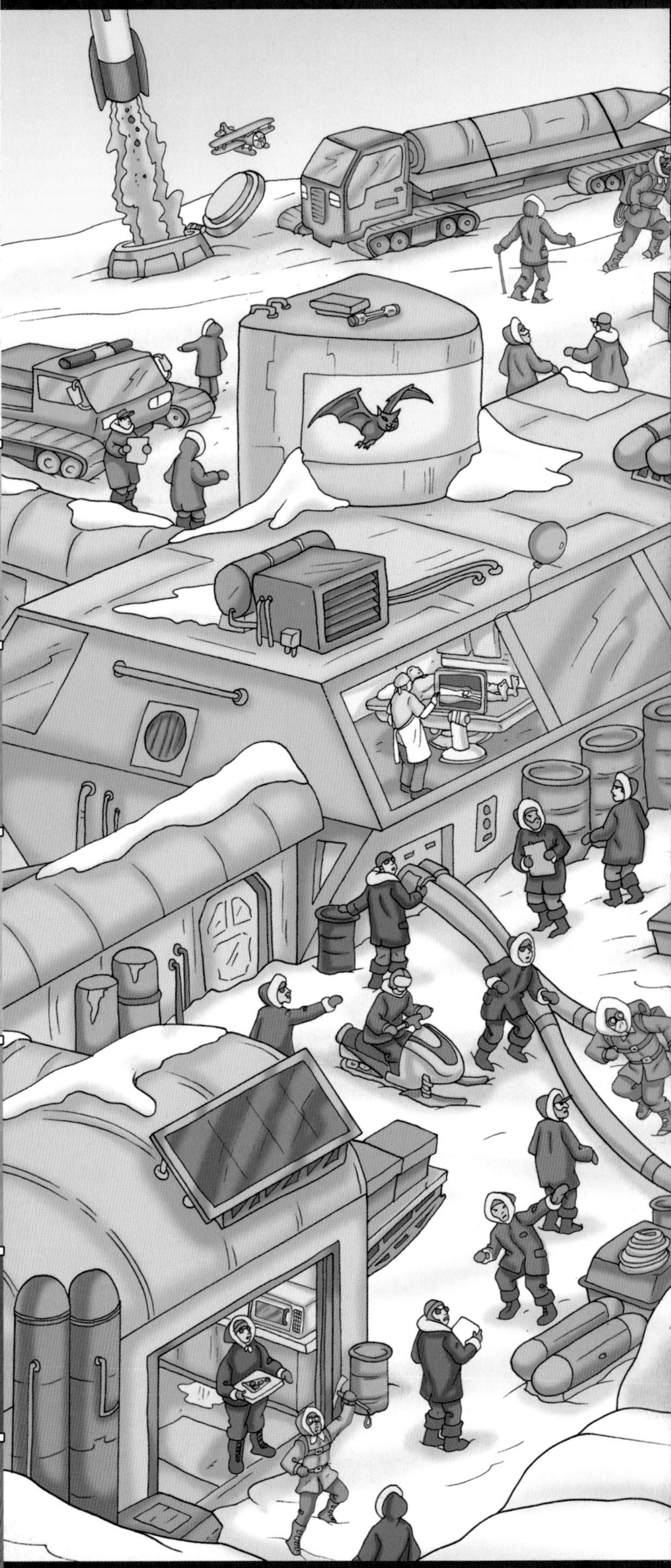

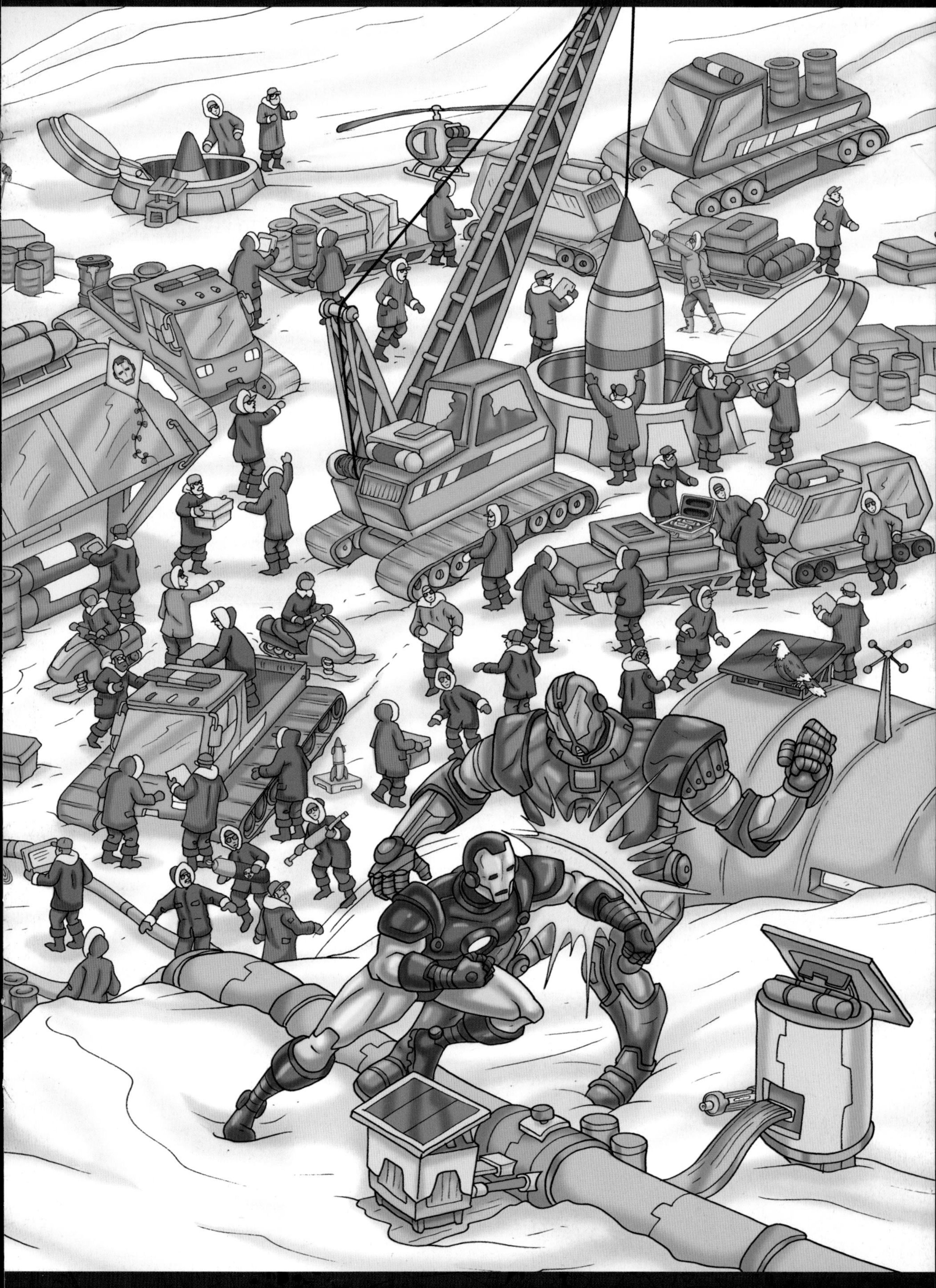

HYDRA HAS USED ITS TECHNOLOGY TO INVENT AN ULTRA-MAGNIFYING GLASS! HARNESSING THE POWER OF THE SUN, THIS WEAPON IS CAPABLE OF ZAPPING ANT-MAN AND WASP FOR GOOD.

AS ANT-MAN MAGNI-FLIES OUT OF HYDRA'S RANGE, FIND THESE HYDRA AGENTS, AND THE OBJECTS CAUGHT IN THEIR MAGNIFYING GLASS'S CROSSBEAMS:

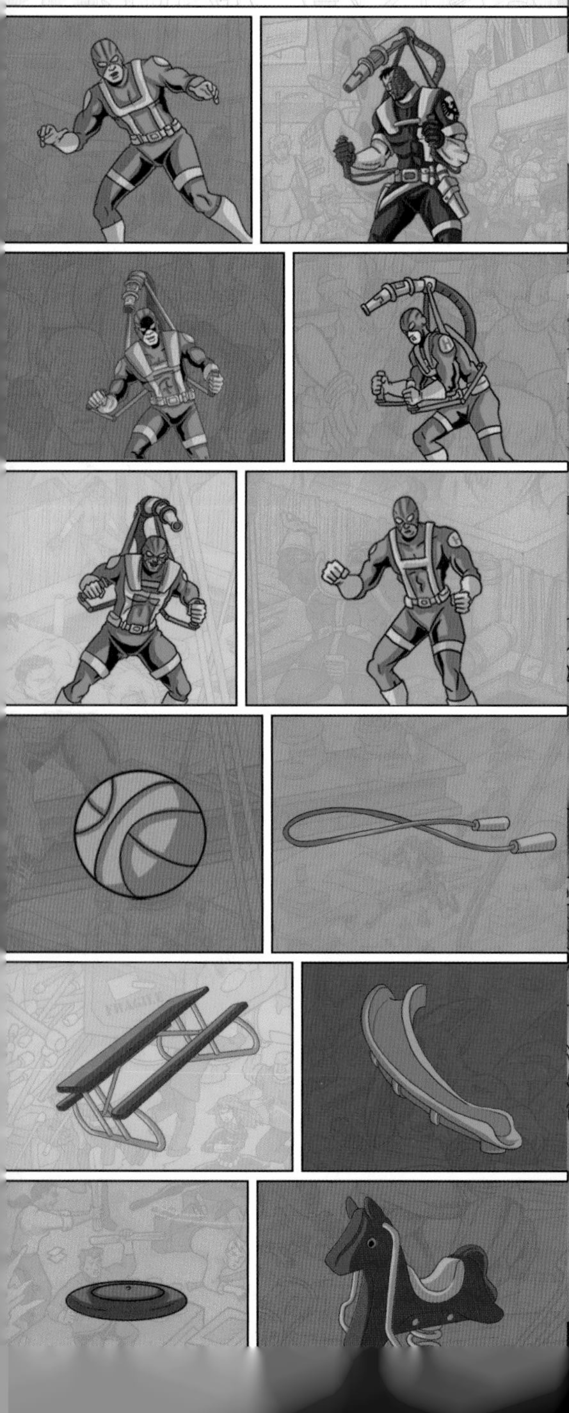

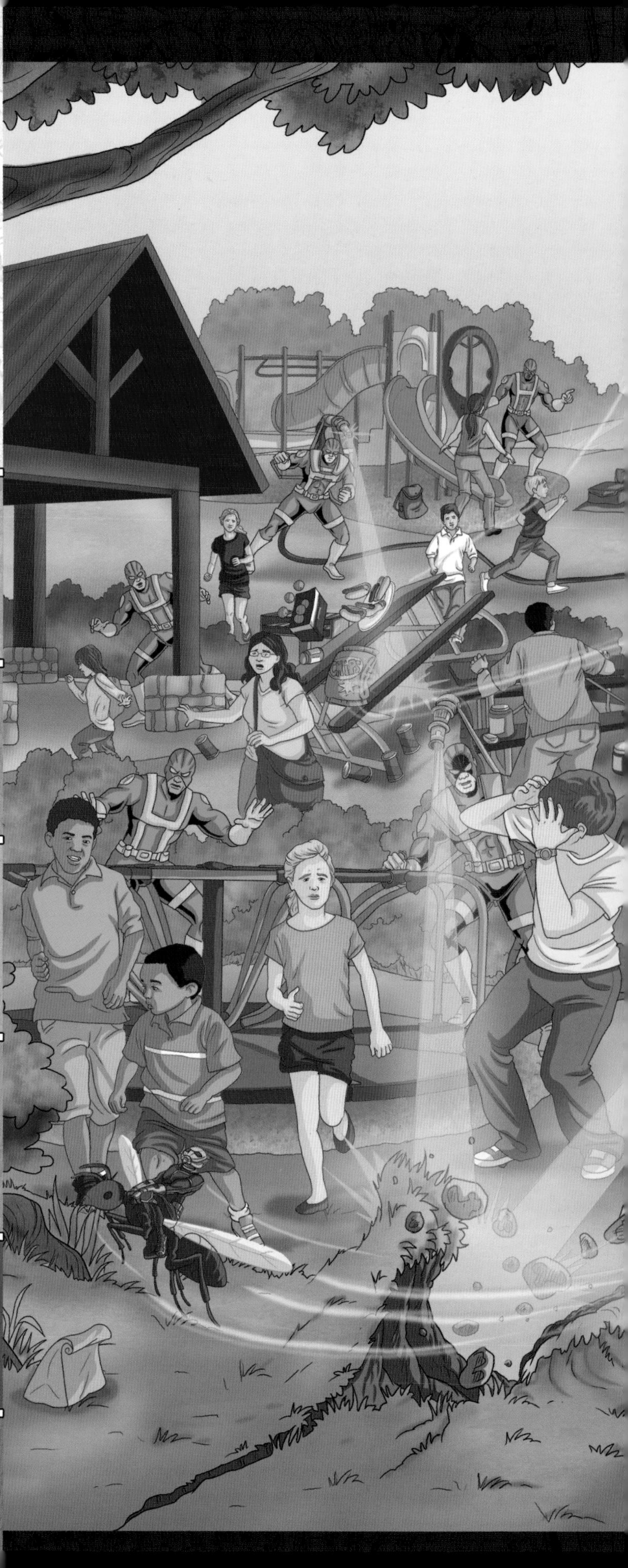

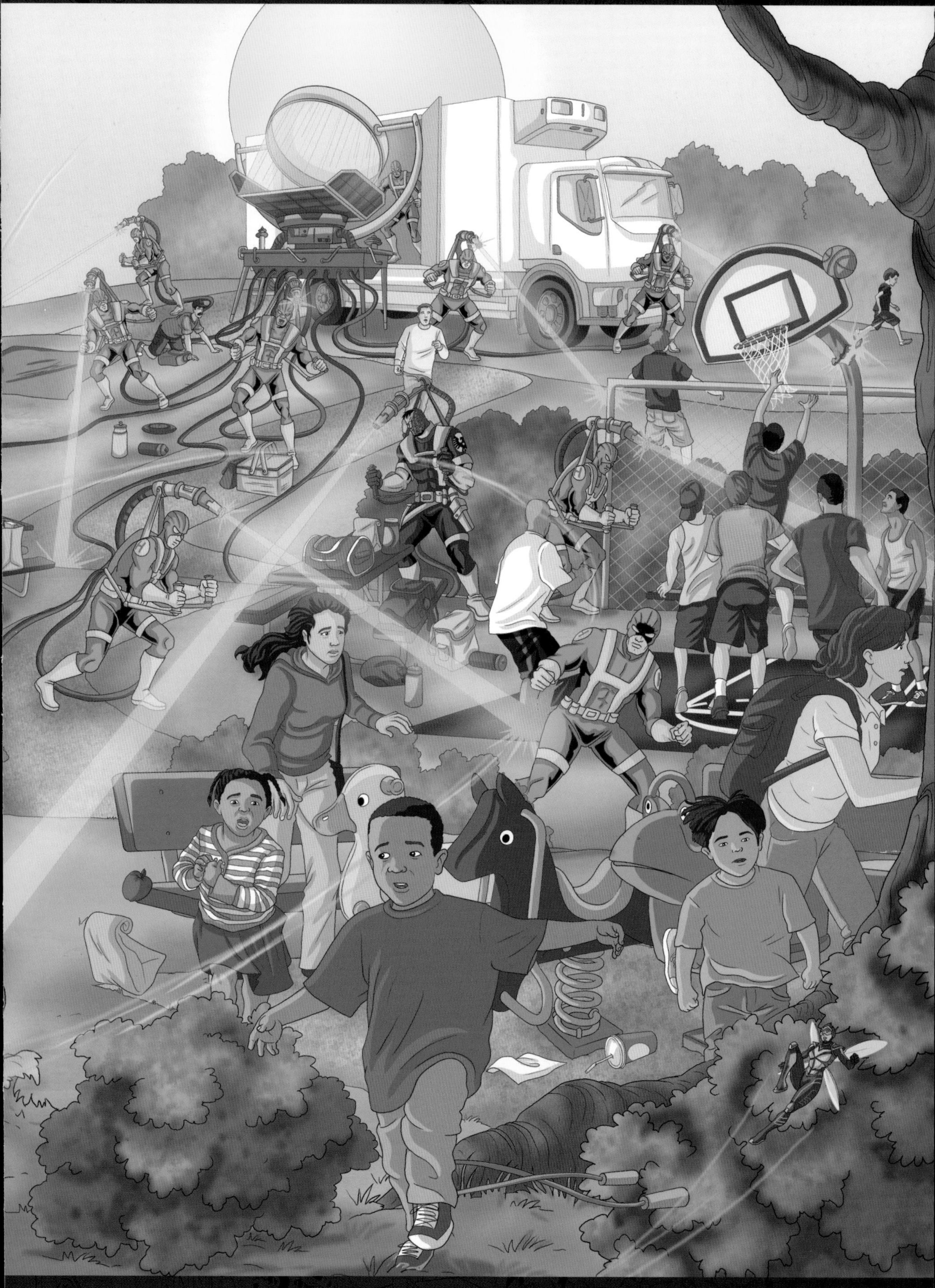

COUNT NEFARIA AND MADAME MASQUE ARE MAKING TROUBLE, AND THEIR GOONS ARE LOOTING THE STREETS OF ROME. THAT'S A LOT FOR IRON MAN TO HANDLE ALONE, BUT LUCKILY THE GUARDIANS OF THE GALAXY ARE IN TOWN, AND THEY DON'T MIND STOPPING IN TO HELP SAVE THE DAY.

HELP MAKE ITALY SAFE BY CATCHING THESE BAD GUYS COMMITTING CRIMES, AND IDENTIFYING THE ITALIAN ART THEY'VE FORGED:

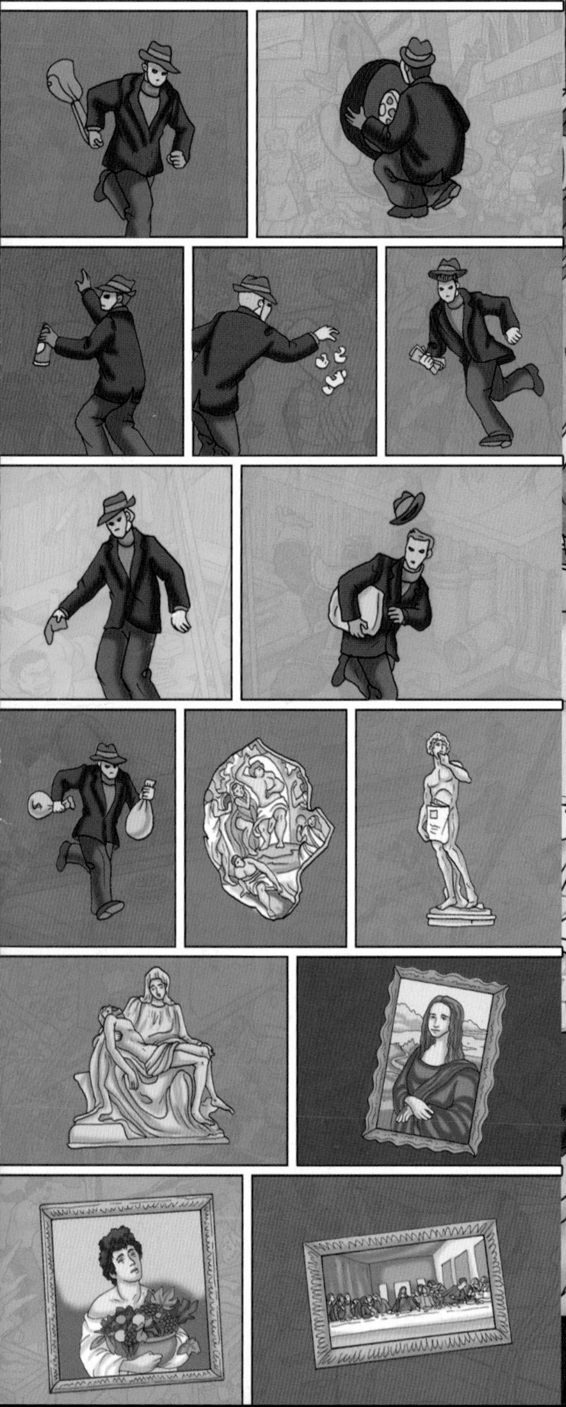

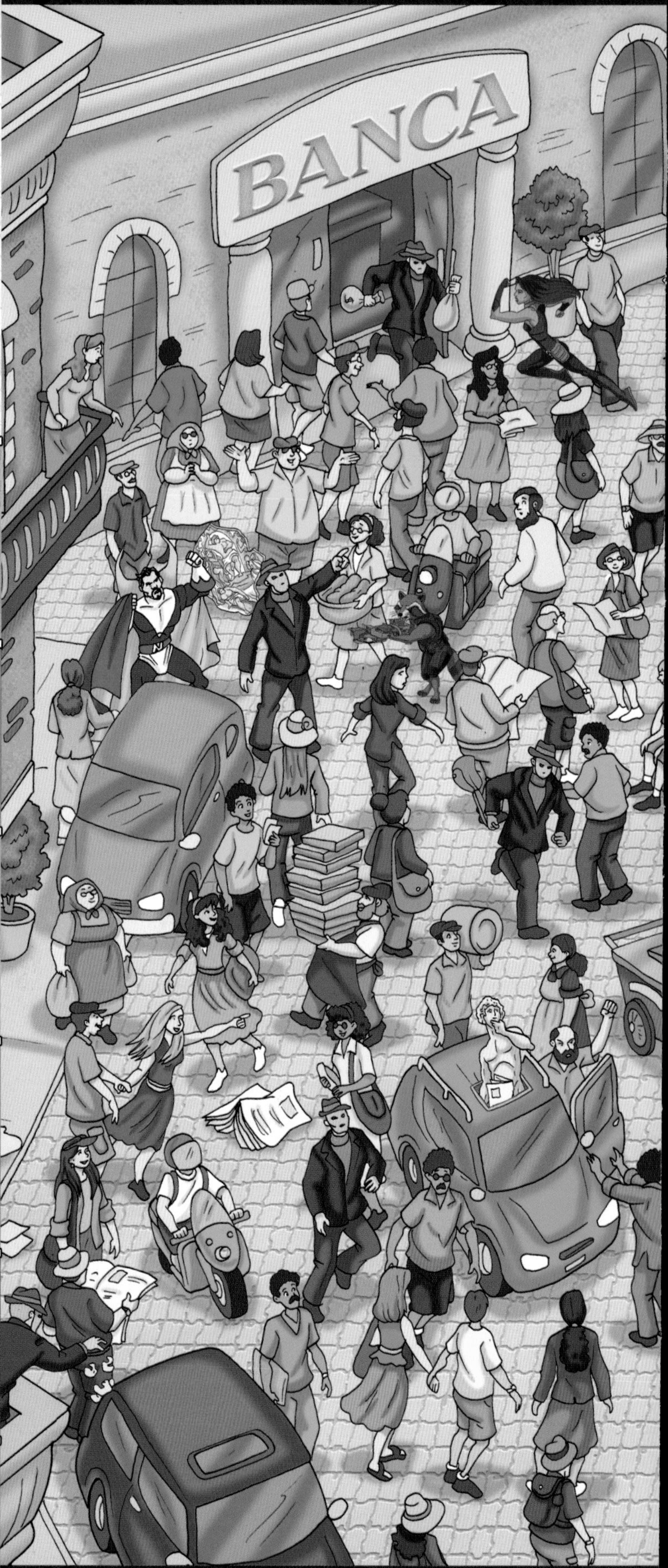
BANCA

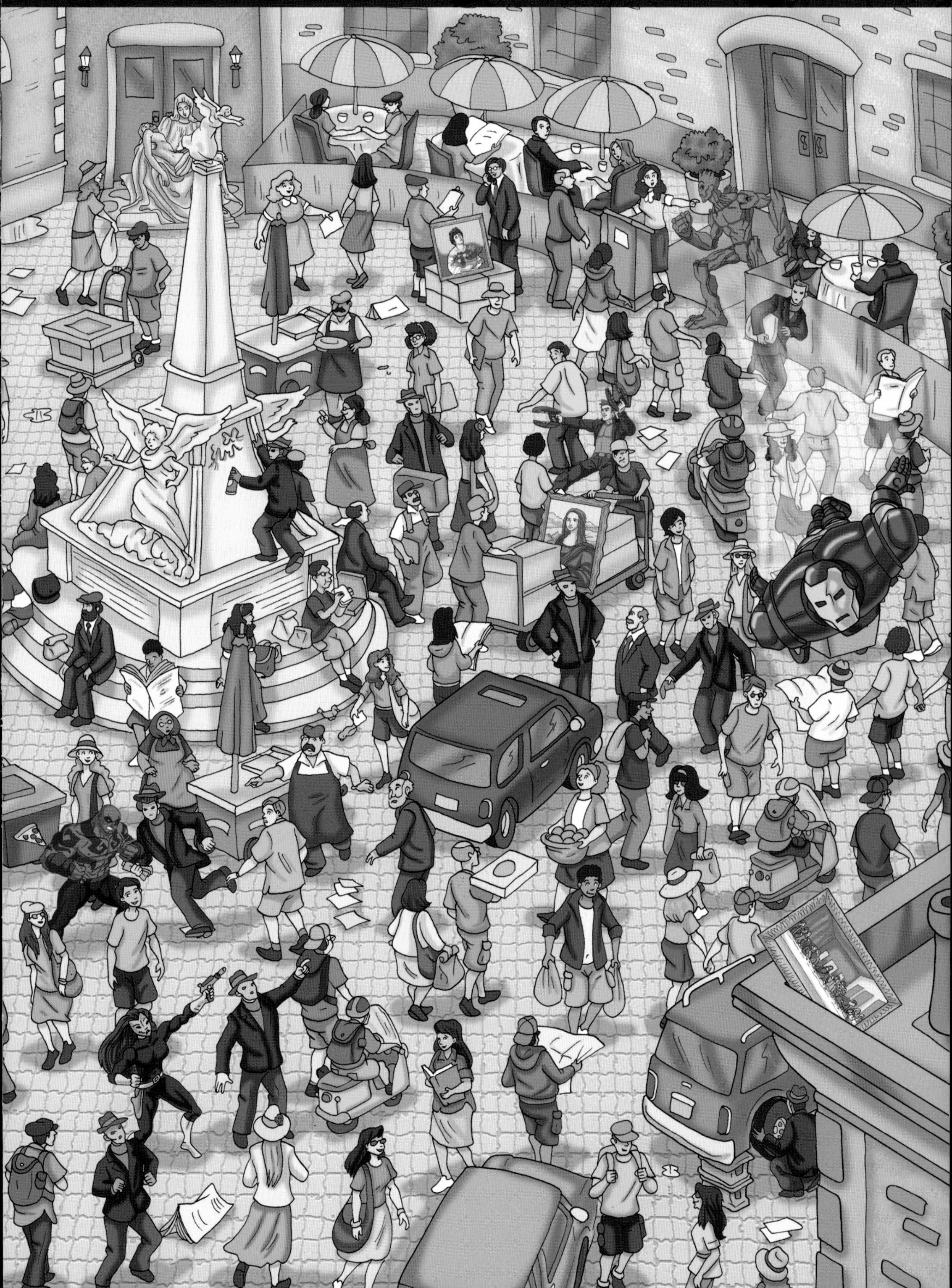

BLACK PANTHER IS CAUGHT BETWEEN A HELICOPTER AND A HARD PLACE! AS HE TAKES ON KLAW'S AIRBORNE EMISSARIES, FALCON SOARS TO HIS RESCUE.

WHILE THE DAUNTLESS DUO DEFENDS WAKANDA, SCAN THE SKIES FOR THESE UNWELCOME FLUNKIES—AND DON'T FORGET TO CHECK THE GROUND FOR FOLIAGE THAT MIGHT BE HIDING MORE HOSTILE HENCHMEN:

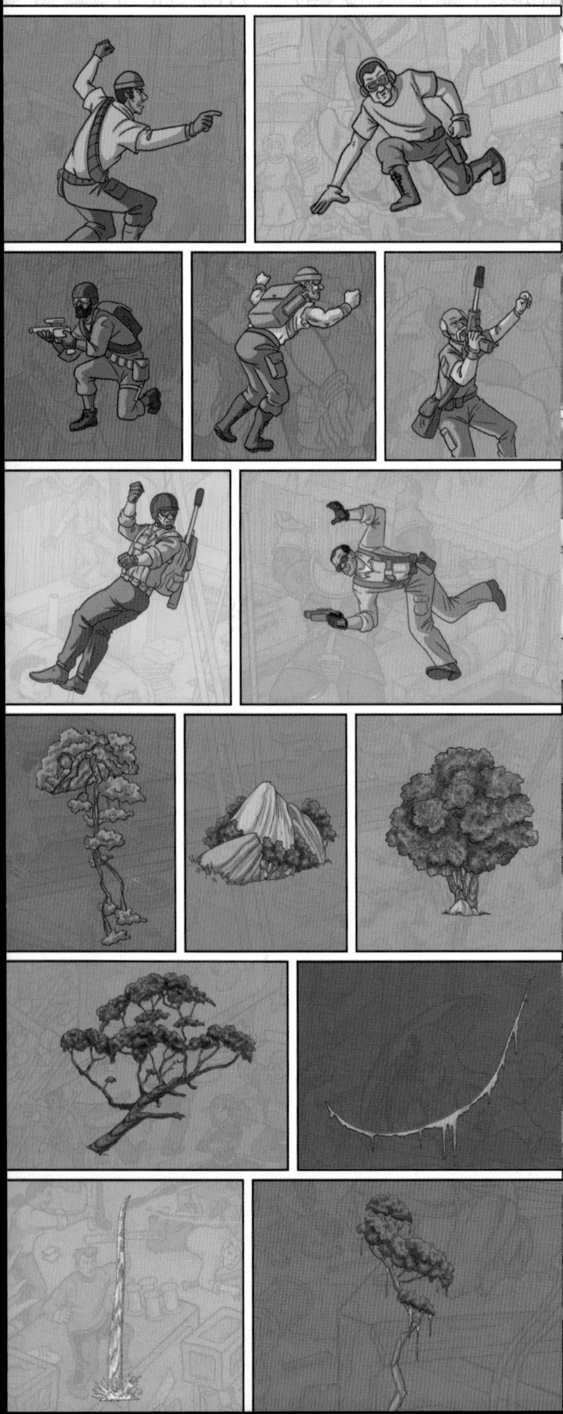

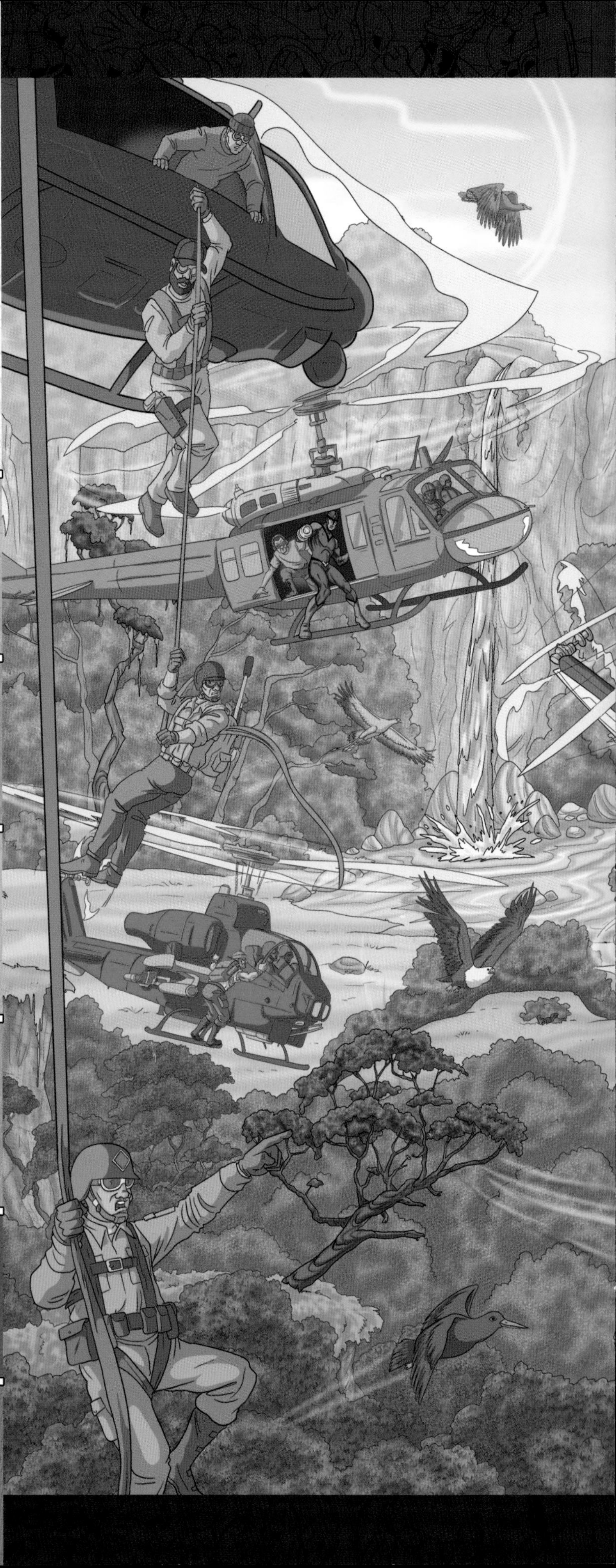

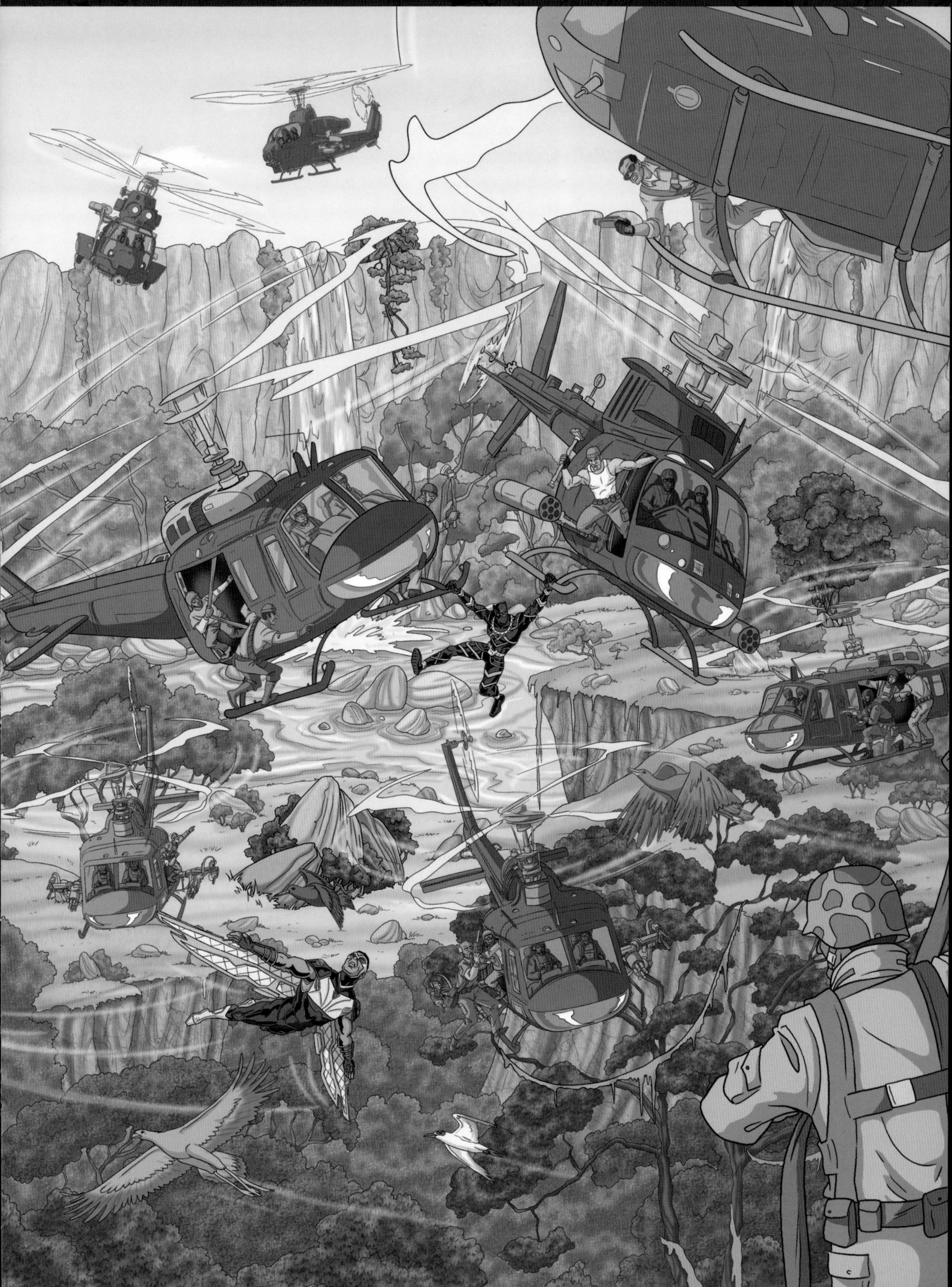

VENOM IS CAUSING A GRIDLOCK! SPIDER-MAN SWINGS OVER TO INVESTIGATE, BUT HE SOON REALIZES KRAVEN HAS LURED HIM INTO A TRAP.

AS KRAVEN HUNTS BOTH HIS ELUSIVE ADVERSARIES, LOOK FOR THESE TYPES OF TRANSPORTATION—AND WATCH OUT FOR THE EIGHT HUNTING SPEARS THAT KRAVEN HAS ALREADY THROWN!

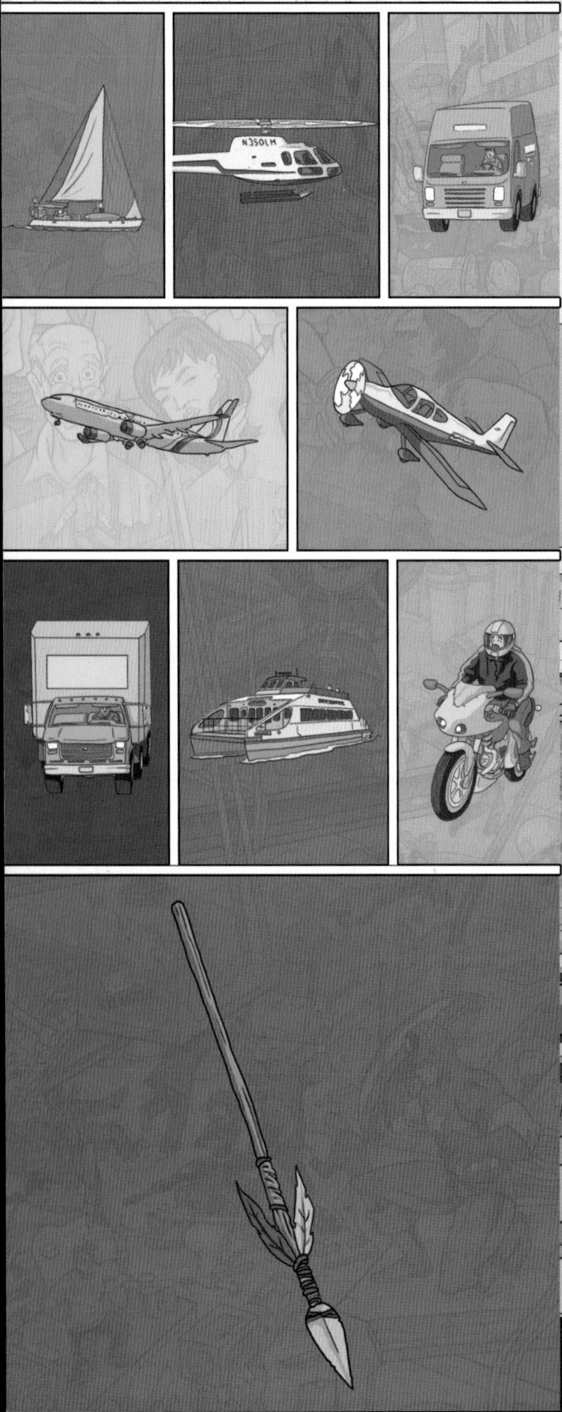

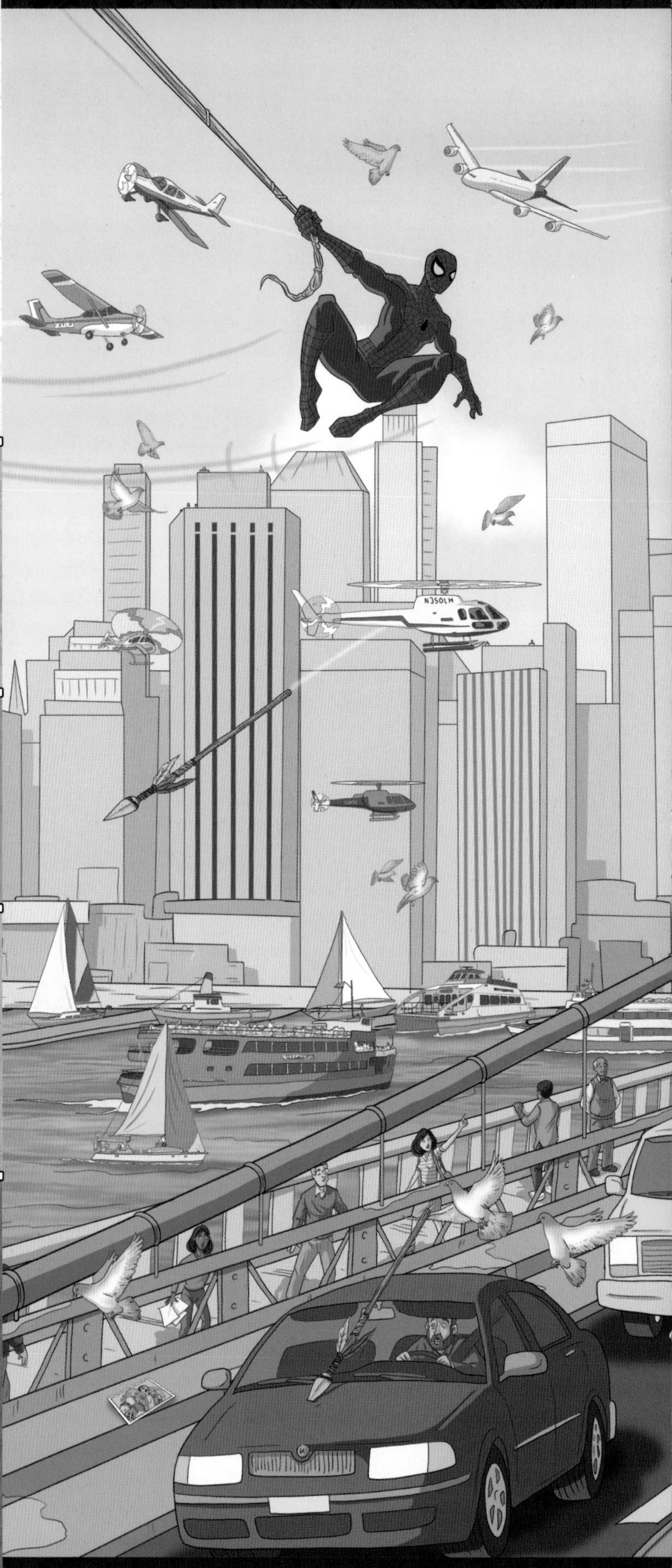

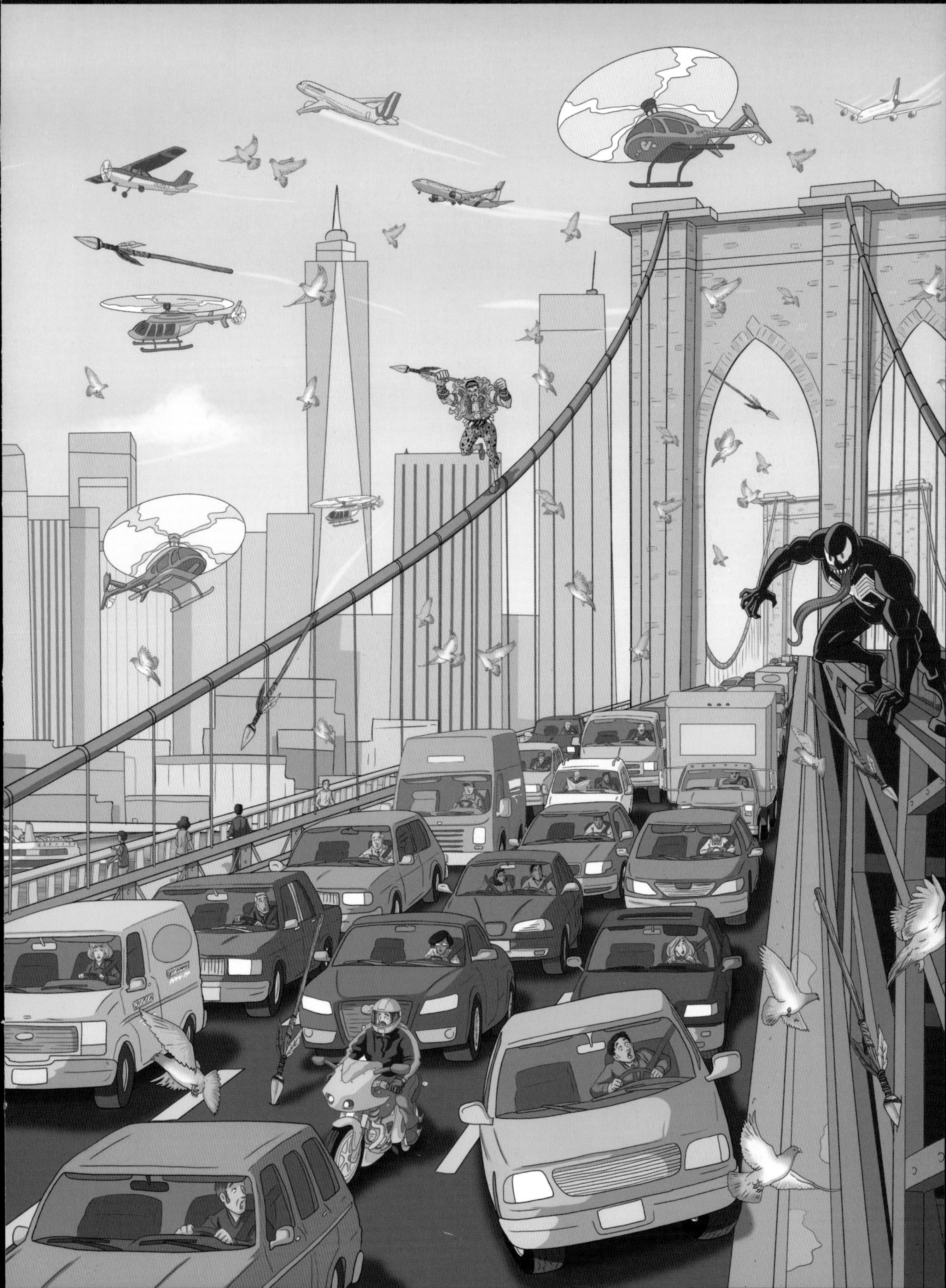

THE AVENGERS NEED SPIDER-MAN'S HELP TO DEFEAT RED SKULL AND HIS ARMY OF HYDRA SOLDIERS.

AS SPIDEY SHOWS THE AVENGERS HOW IT'S DONE, LOOK AROUND FOR THINGS THAT RED SKULL MIGHT USE AGAINST THE HEROES, AND SIX HYDRA LOGOS MARKING HIS MINIONS:

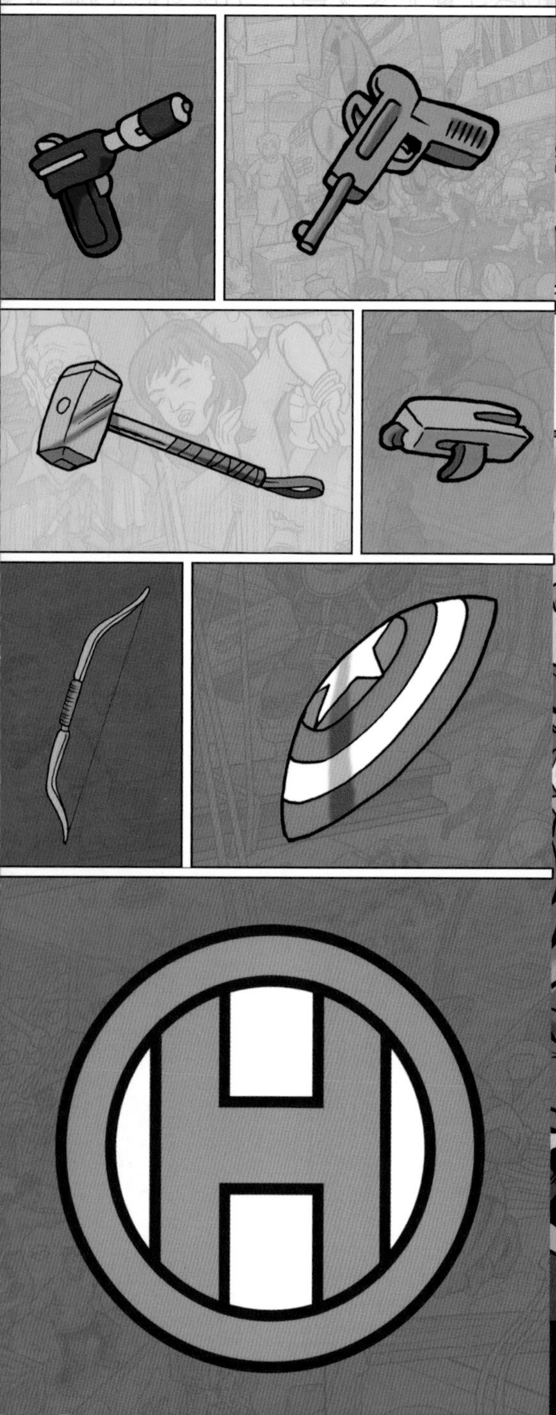

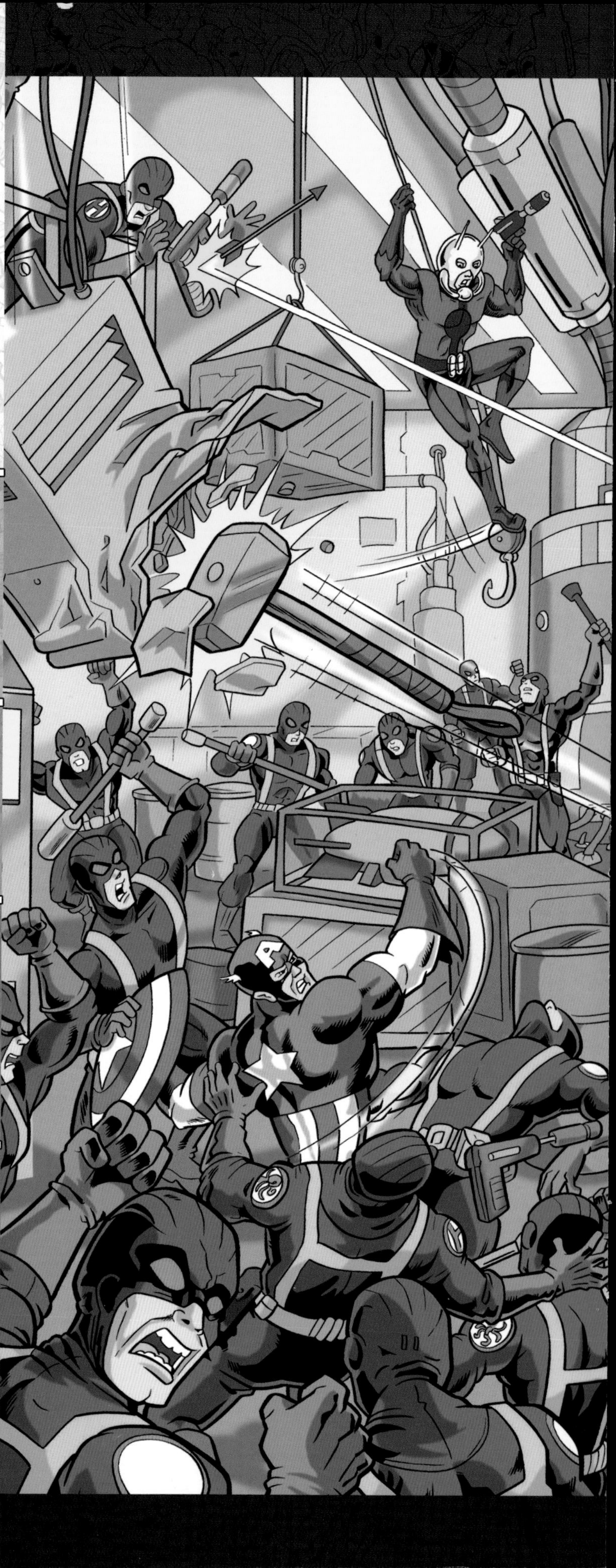

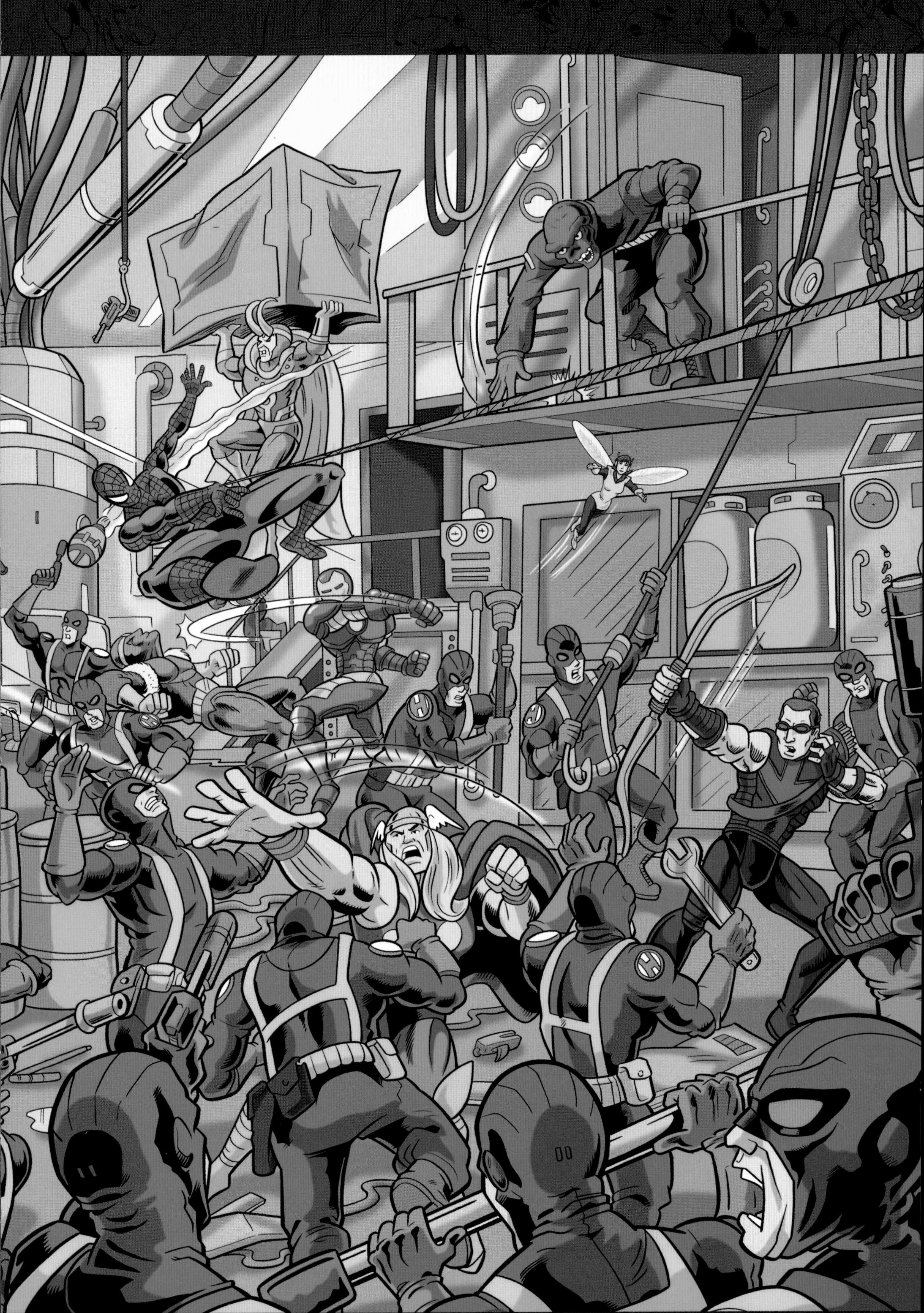

THERE'S SOMETHING WRONG AT STARK INDUSTRIES. THE GHOST, A THIEVING SUPER VILLAIN, HAS BEEN HIRED BY ONE OF TONY STARK'S ENEMIES TO STEAL HIS IRON MAN TECHNOLOGY. BUT STARK PUTS ON HIS ARMOR TO STOP THE BAD GUY.

WHILE IRON MAN PUTS UP A FIGHT, FIND THESE THINGS THE GHOST WANTS TO SWIPE, AND THE FRIGHTENED EMPLOYEES IRON MAN NEEDS TO PROTECT:

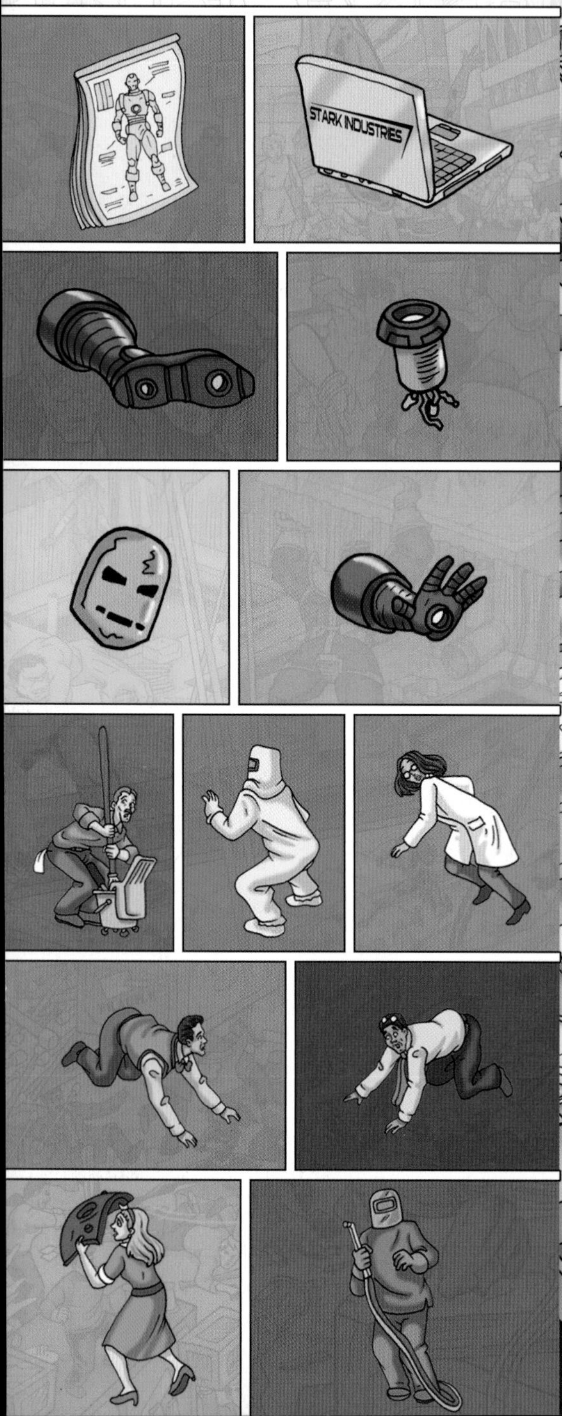
STARK INDUSTRIES

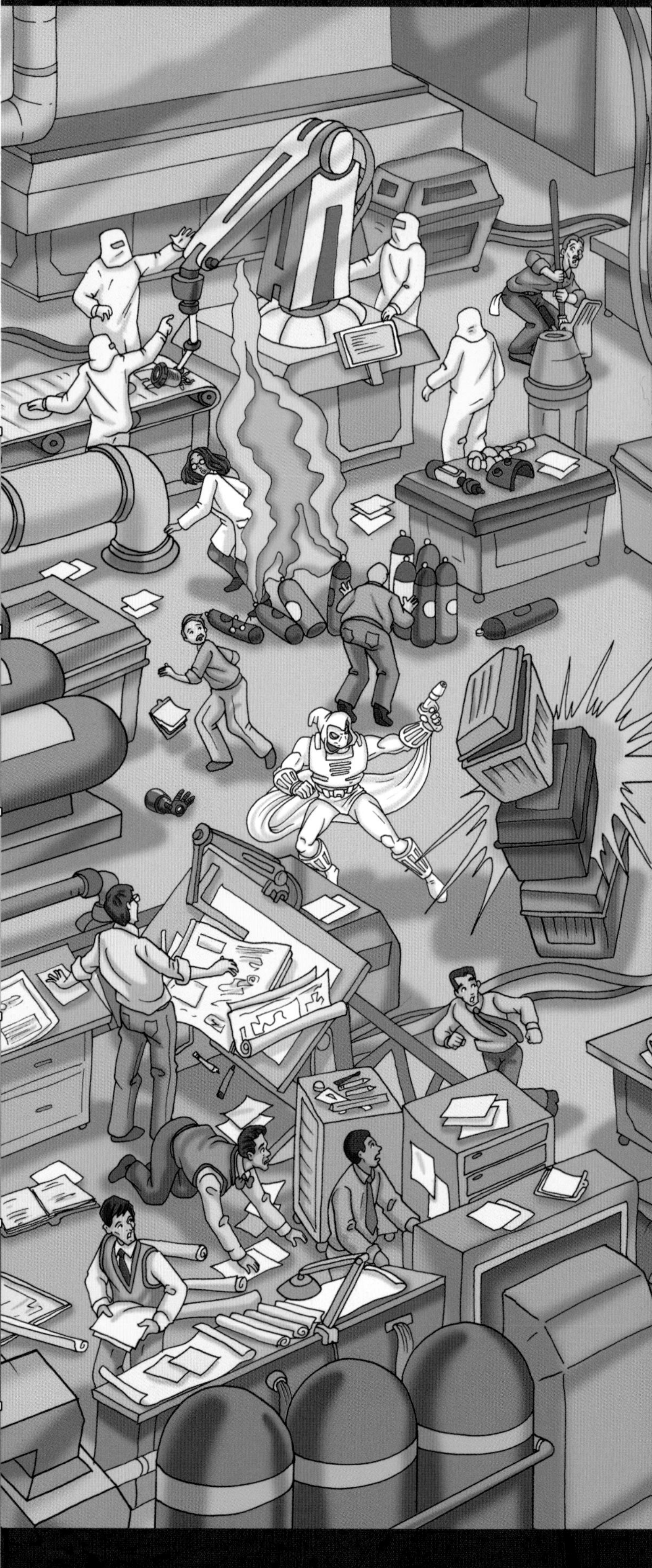

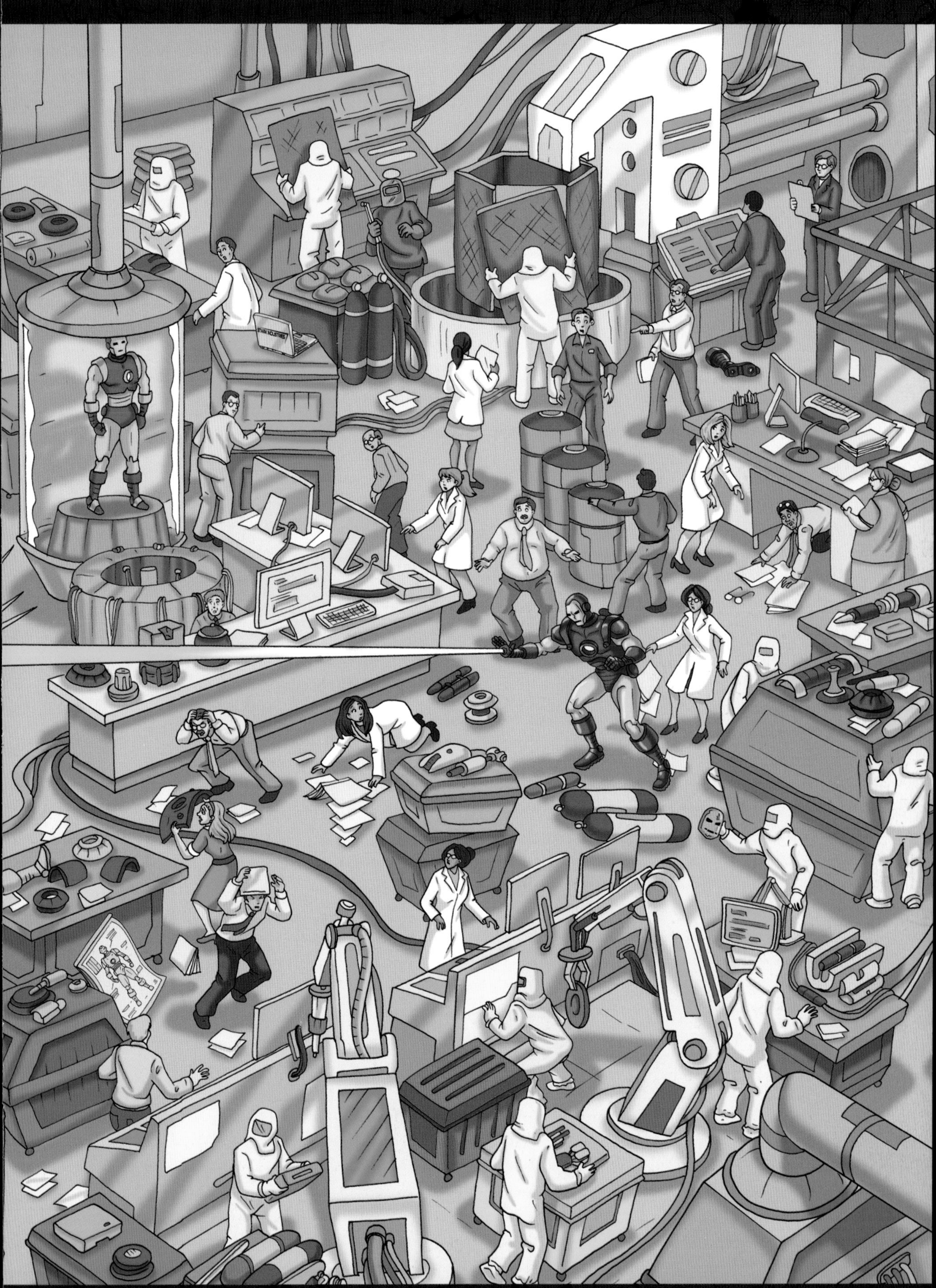
STARK INDUSTRIES

ROCKET AND GROOT'S LATEST MISSION HAS LED THEM TO PLANET X—GROOT'S HOME PLANET. GROOT WAS EXILED FROM PLANET X YEARS AGO, AND HIS HERBACEOUS BROTHERS WON'T LET HIM FORGET IT.

AS THE PANICKED PAIR HIGHTAILS IT BACK TO ROCKET'S SHIP, FIND A FEW FLORAL FEATURES AND THESE HOSTILE GROOT LOOKALIKES:

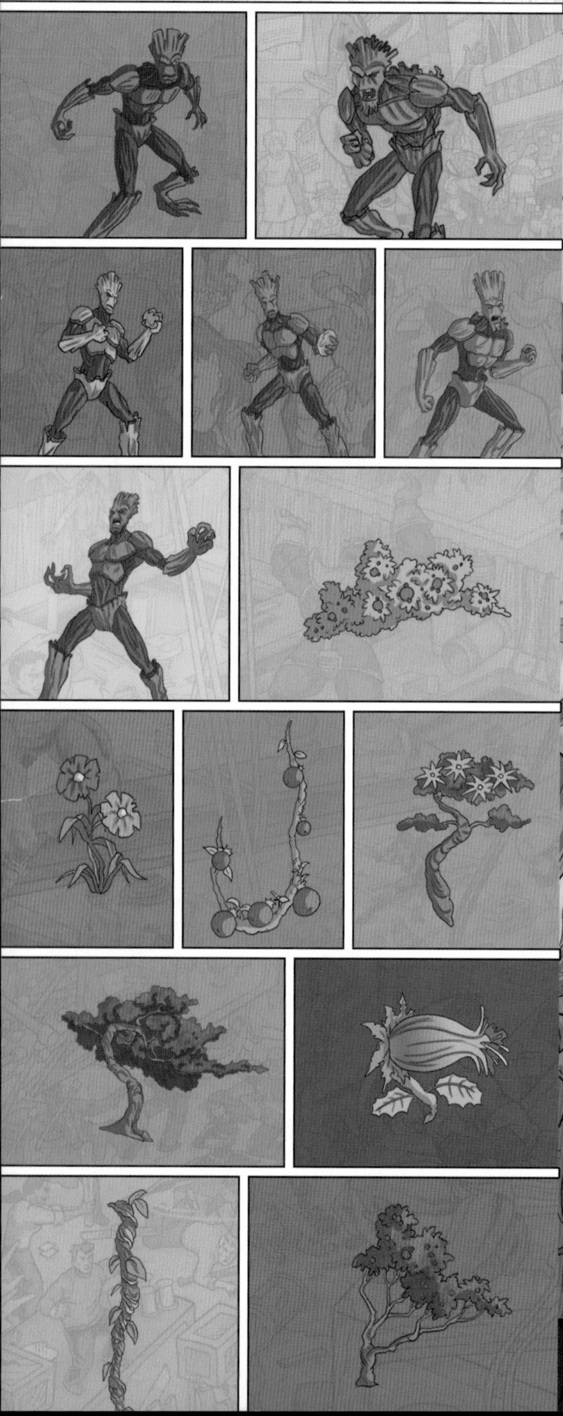

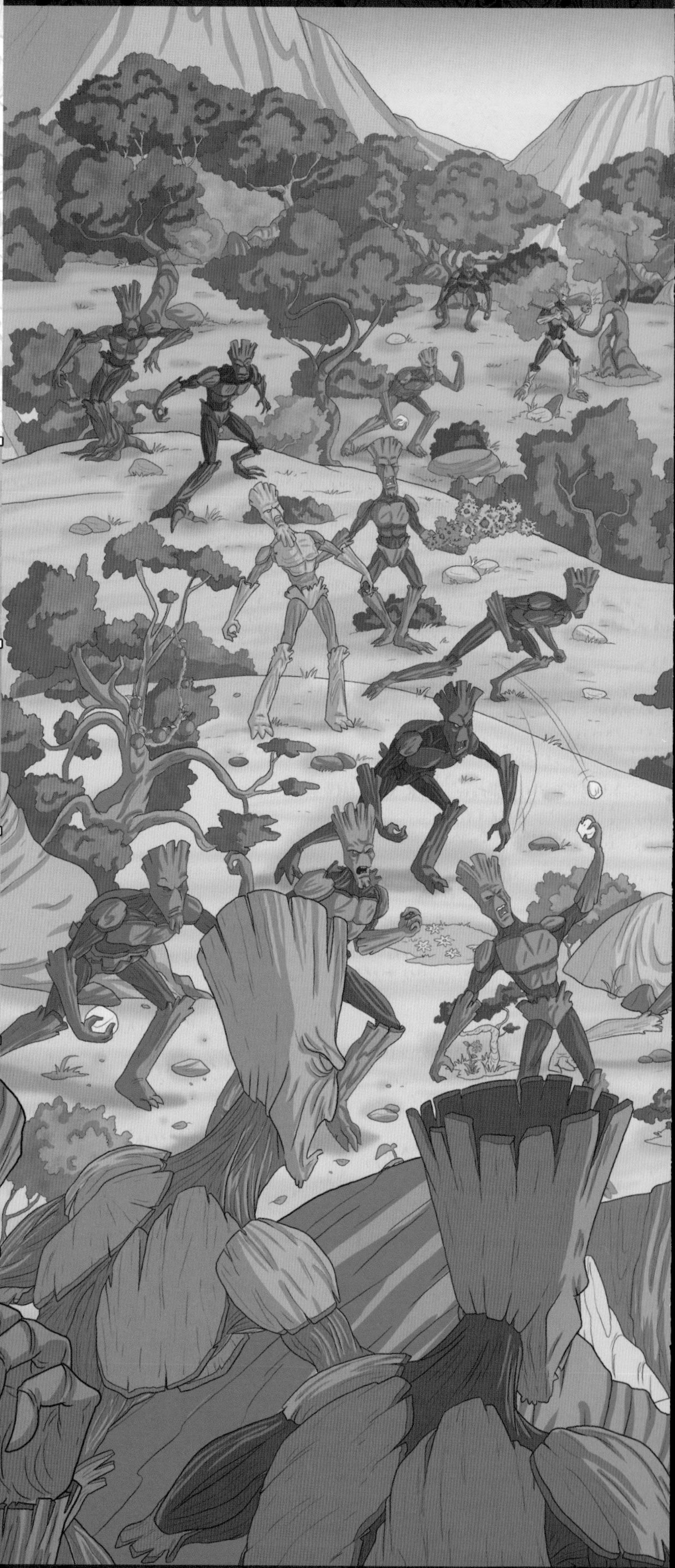

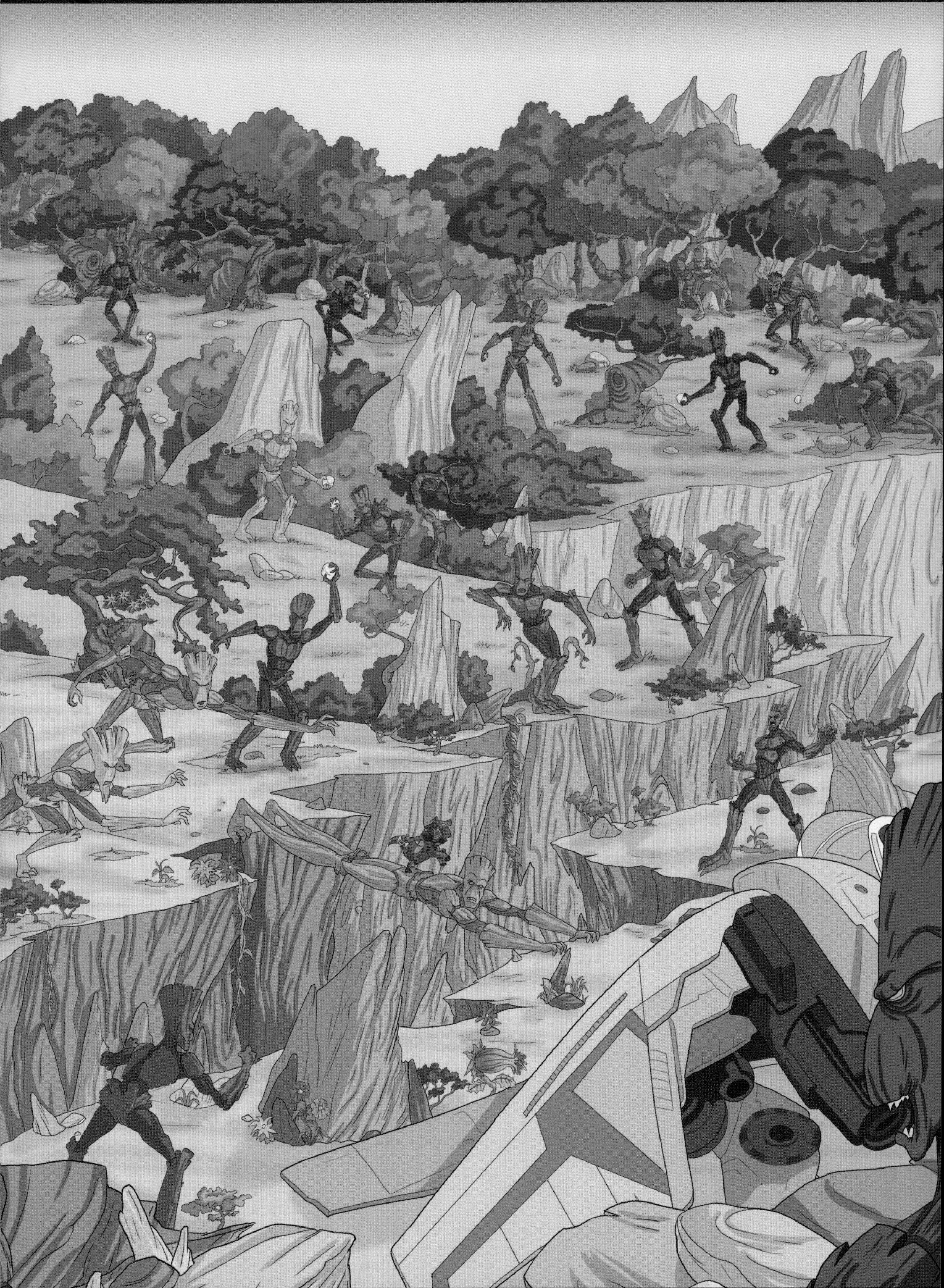

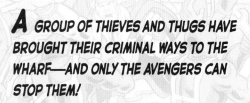

A GROUP OF THIEVES AND THUGS HAVE BROUGHT THEIR CRIMINAL WAYS TO THE WHARF—AND ONLY THE AVENGERS CAN STOP THEM!

SIFT THROUGH THE ACTION AND FIND OUR HEROES, THEN HELP THEM SPOT THE VILLAINS AND OTHER THINGS LURKING AROUND THE DOCKS:

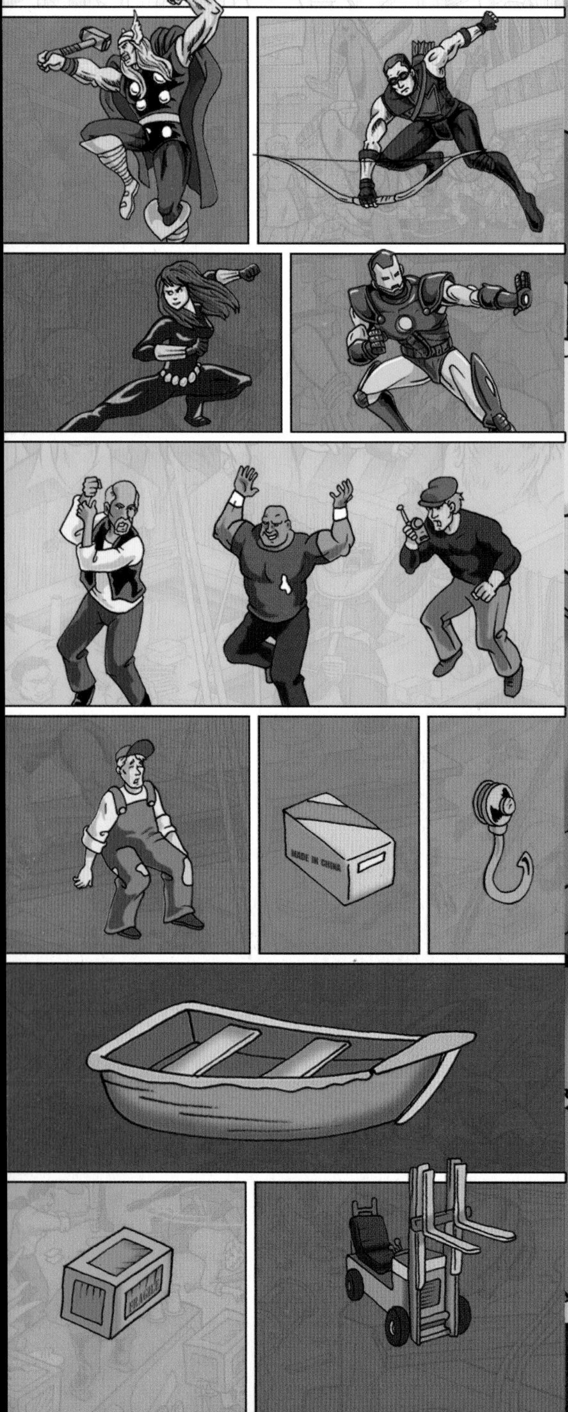

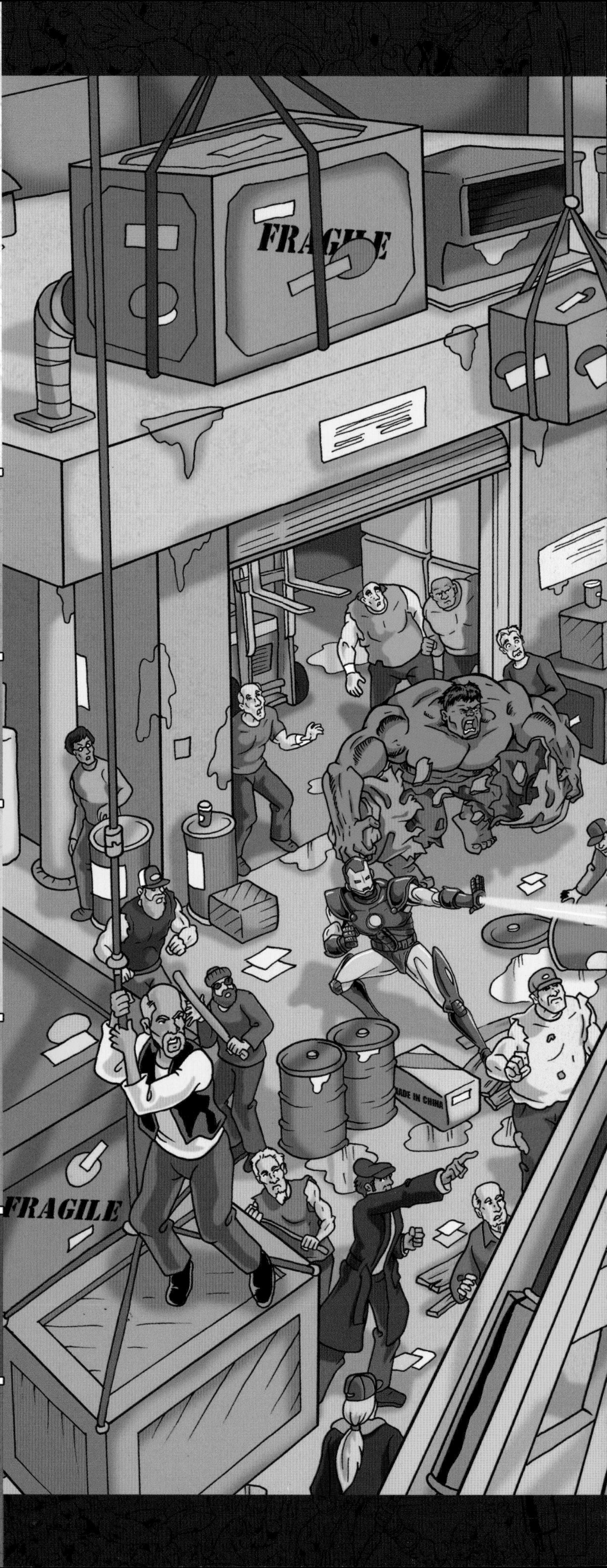
FRAGILE
MADE IN CHINA
FRAGILE

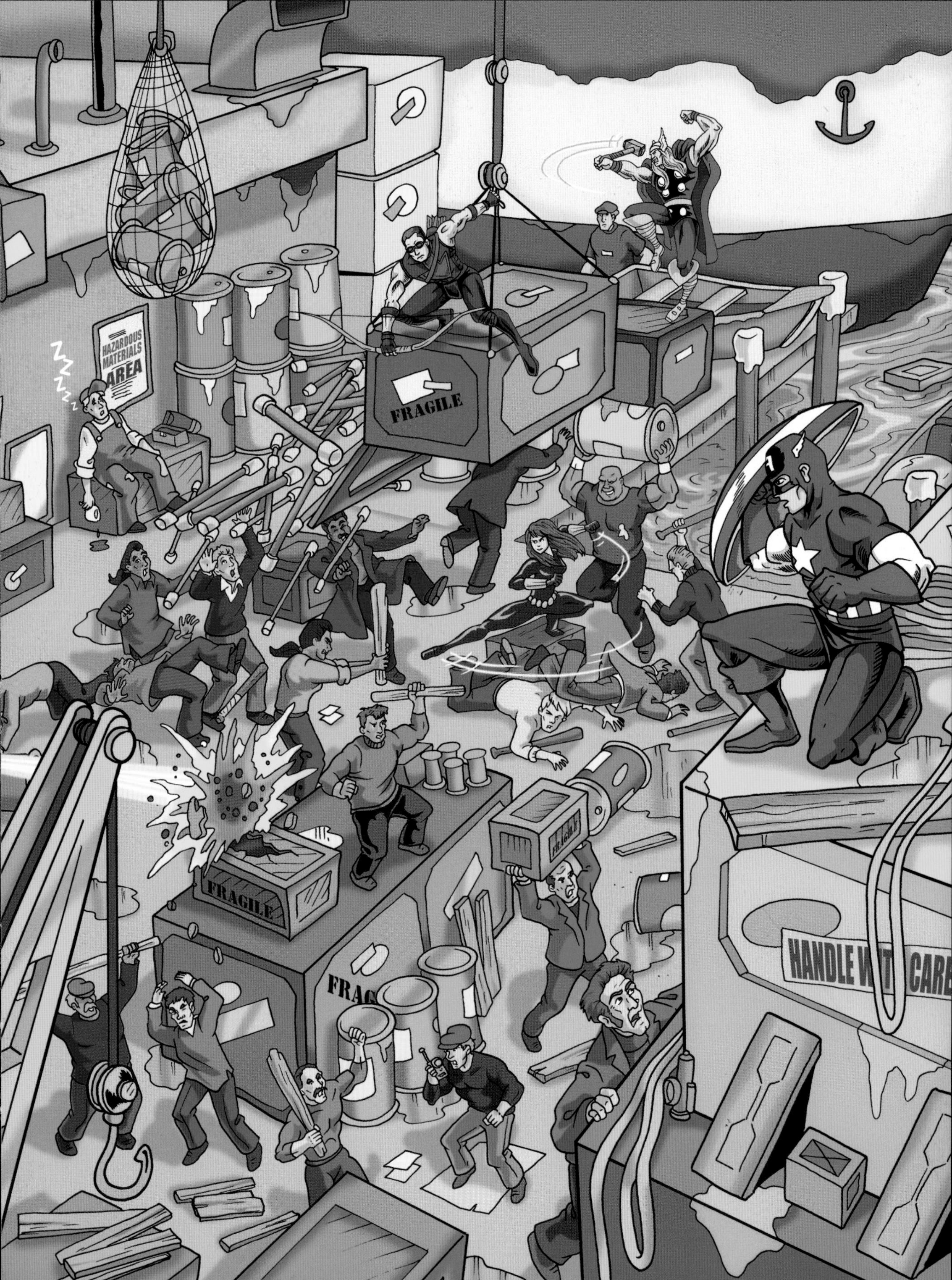
HAZARDOUS MATERIALS AREA
FRAGILE
FRAGILE
FRAGILE
FRAG
HANDLE WITH CARE

PETER PARKER HAS PICTURES TO TAKE FOR THE *DAILY BUGLE*...AND WHAT BETTER WAY TO GET THE PHOTOS THAN BY FIGHTING THE CRIME FRONT AND CENTER? IN PERFECT TIMING, ELECTRO HAS JUST EMERGED, AND HE'S TRYING TO ABSORB THE ELECTRICITY FROM THE SUBWAY SYSTEM!

LOOK OUT FOR ELECTRO'S ERRATIC BOLTS OF ELECTRICITY AS YOU HELP THESE TRANSIT-TAKERS AVOID THE VICIOUS VOLTAGE:

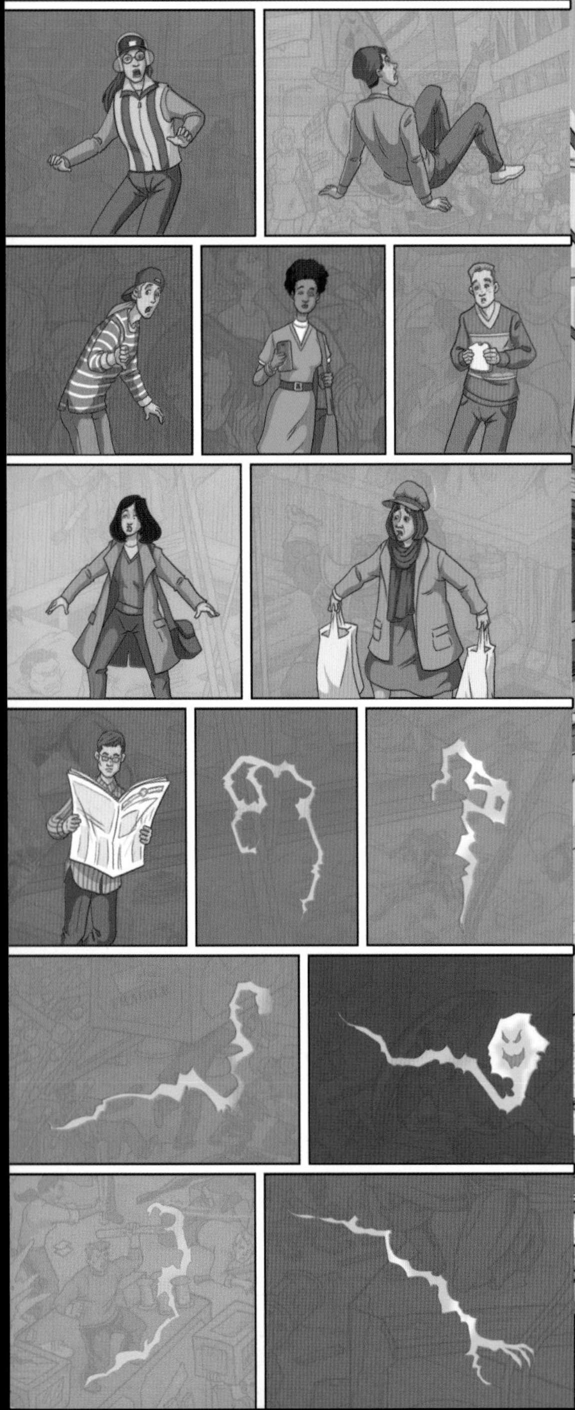

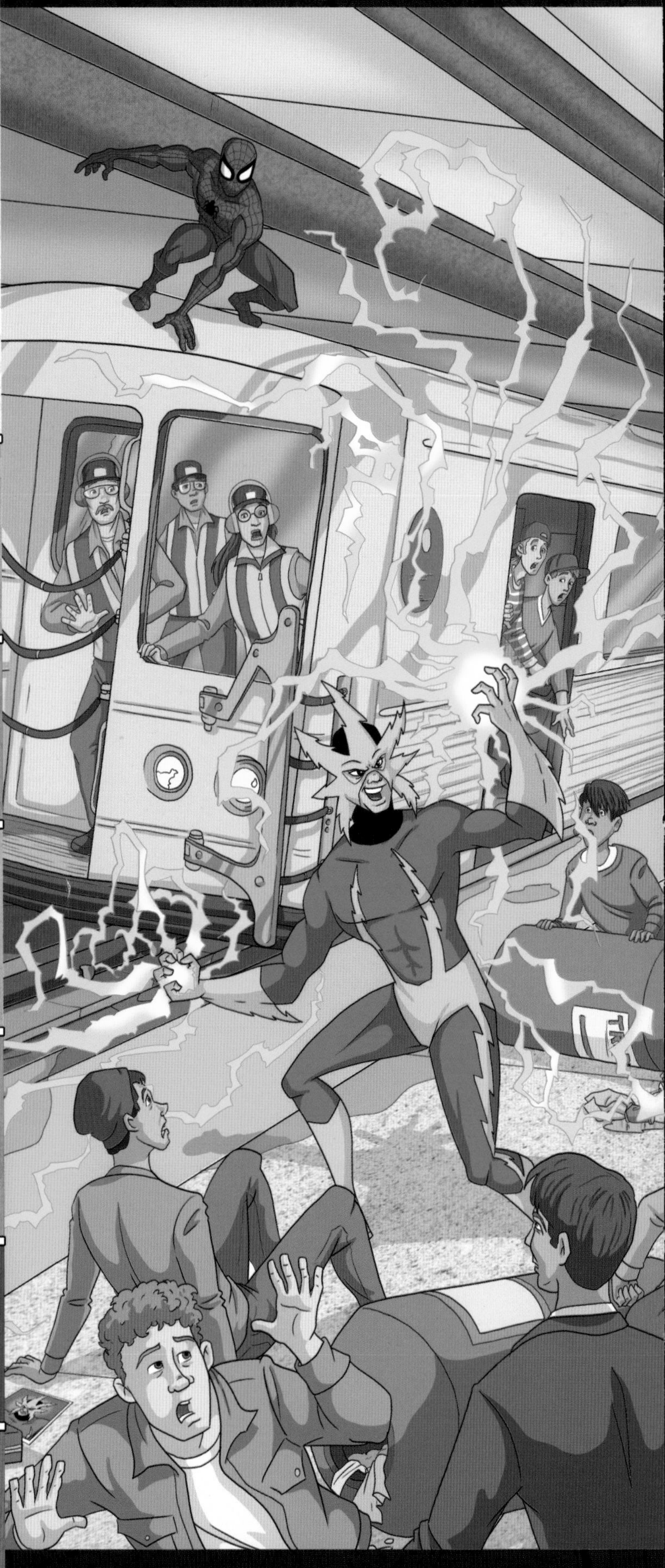

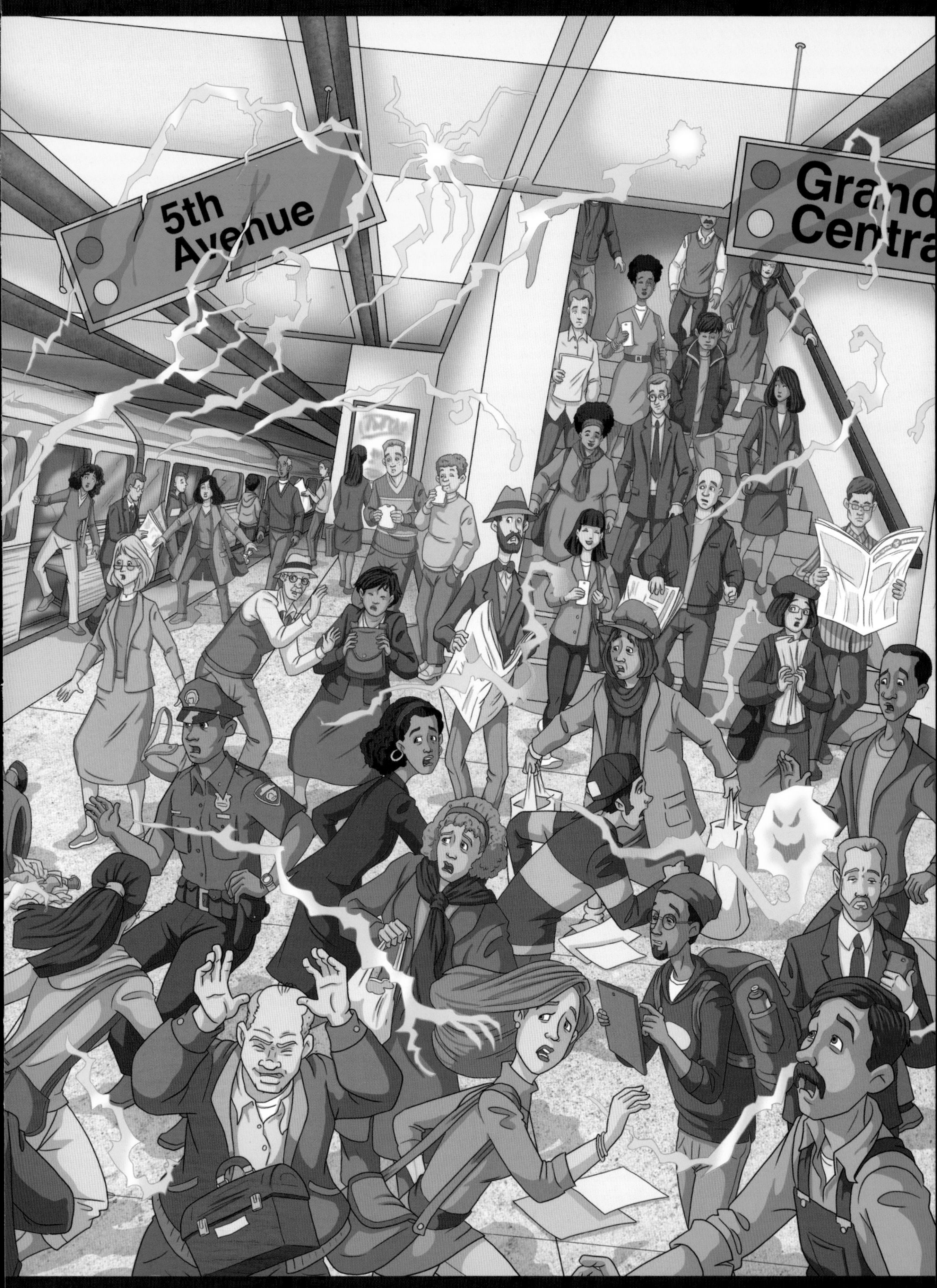
5th
Avenue
Grand
Centra

WHIPLASH IS WREAKING HAVOC ON MOSCOW! IRON MAN STEPS IN TO DEFEND THE CITY.

WHILE THESE TWO DAREDEVILS DUKE IT OUT, SPOT THINGS THAT WHIPLASH HAS TORN IN HALF WITH HIS ENERGY WHIPS, AND HELP IRON MAN FIND THESE EVIL UNDERLINGS, DESPITE THEIR DISGUISES:

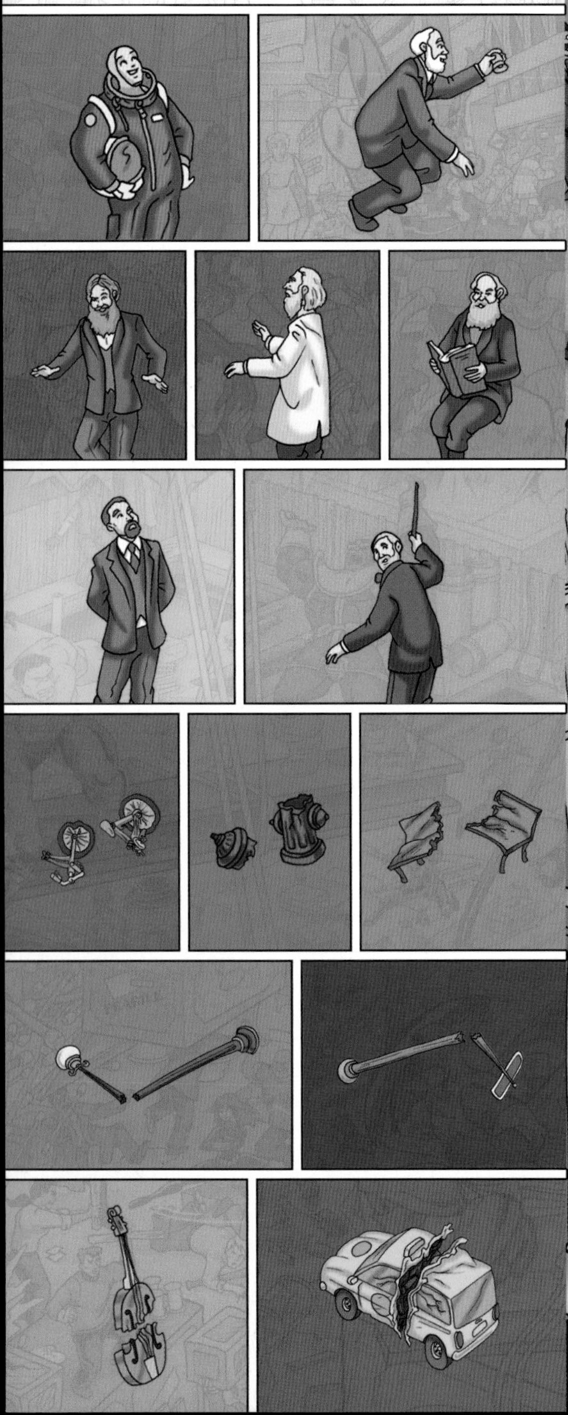

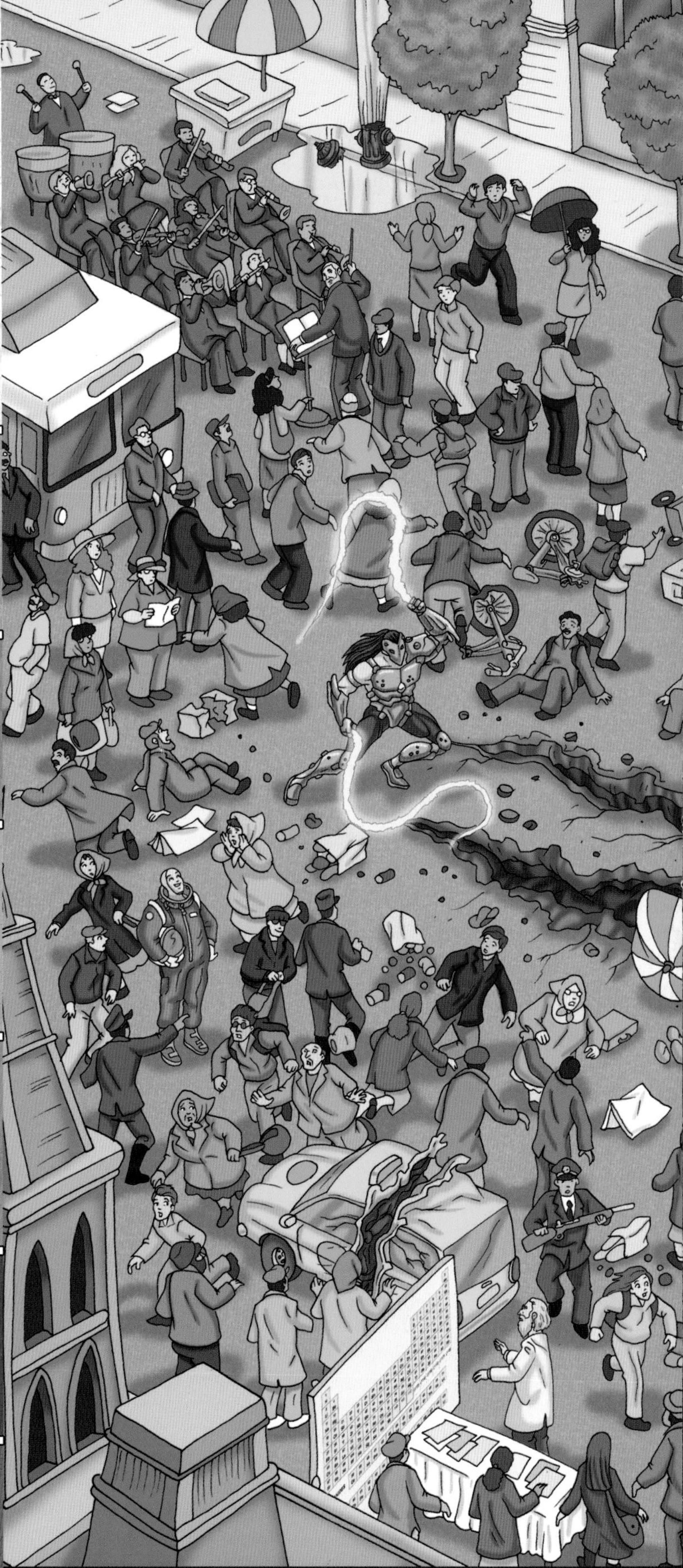

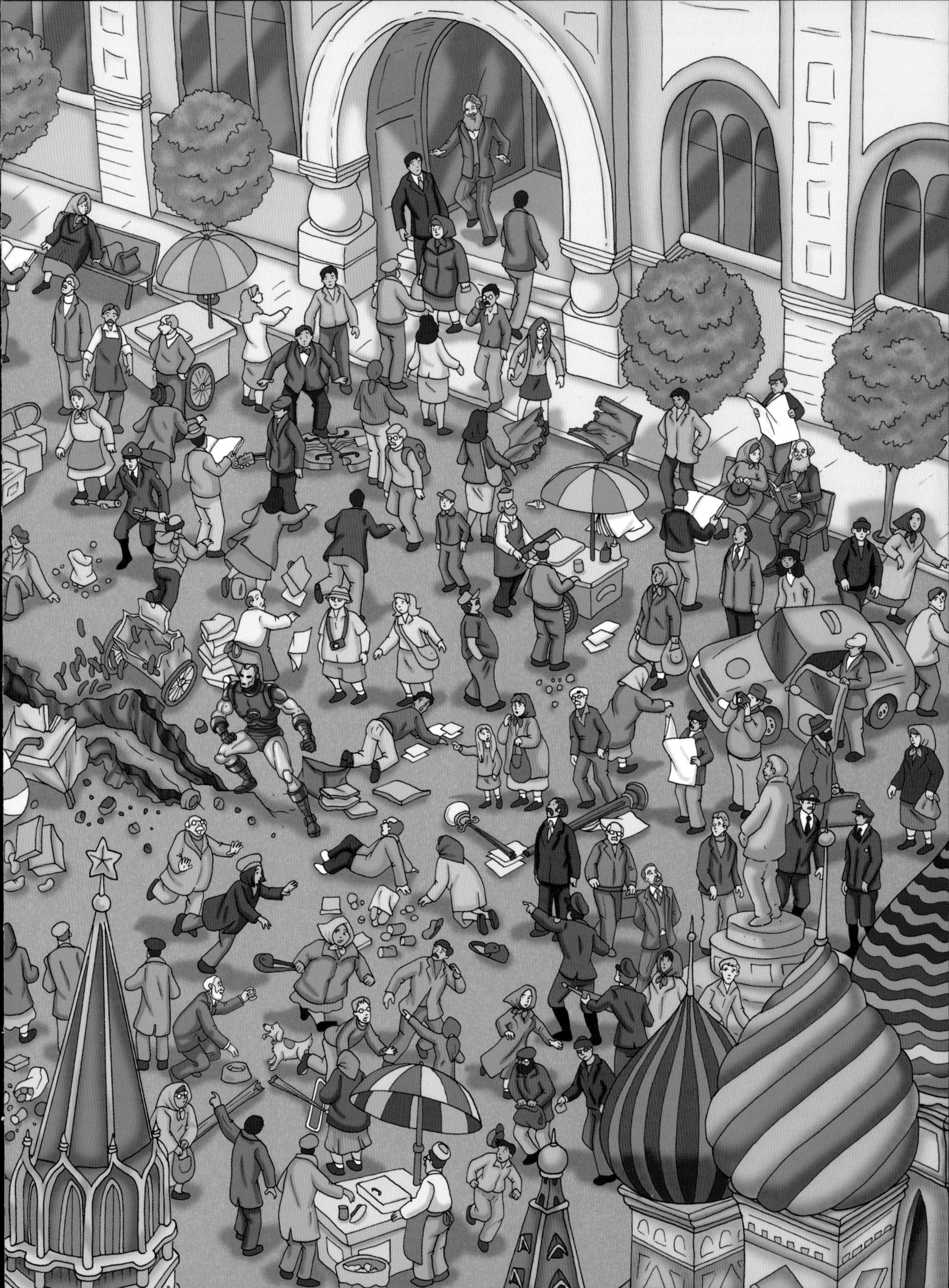

IN NEW YORK CITY, THERE ARE SO MANY WORKERS WHO HELP KEEP THINGS IN ORDER. BUT WHEN CHAOS BREAKS OUT, IT'S SPIDER-MAN TO THE RESCUE!

WHILE SPIDEY AND FRIENDS FIGHT OFF THE BAD GUYS, SEARCH THE STREETS FOR THESE TRAFFIC SIGNS AND CIVIL SERVANTS:

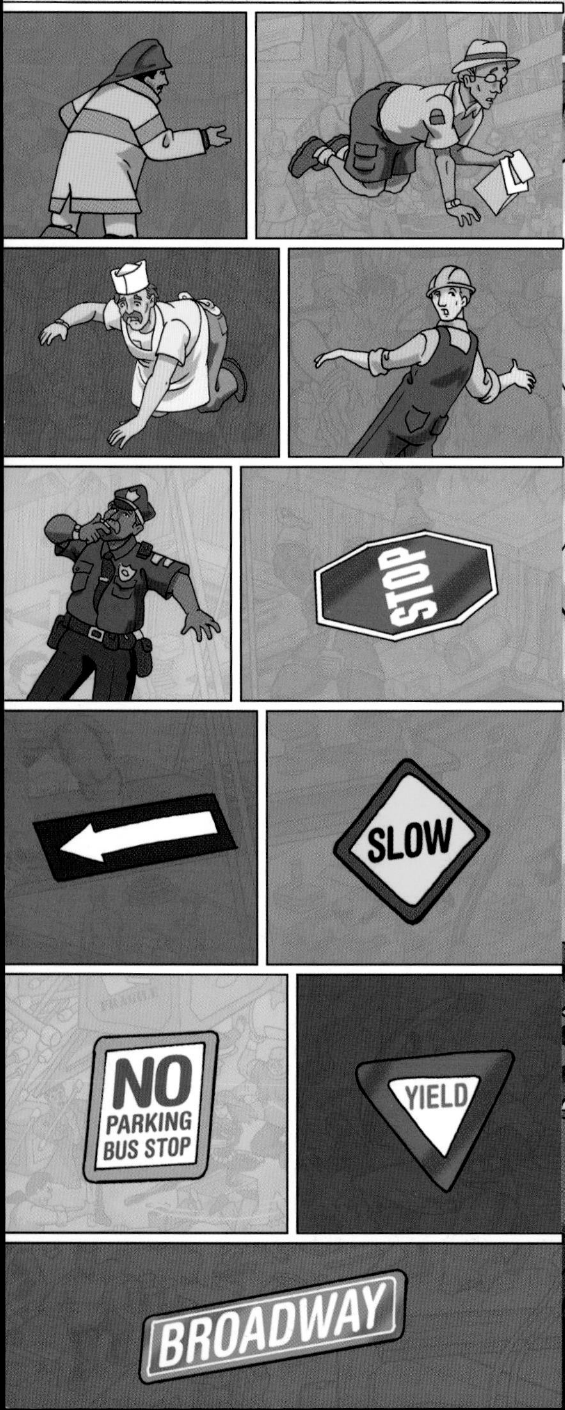
STOP
SLOW
NO PARKING BUS STOP
YIELD
BROADWAY

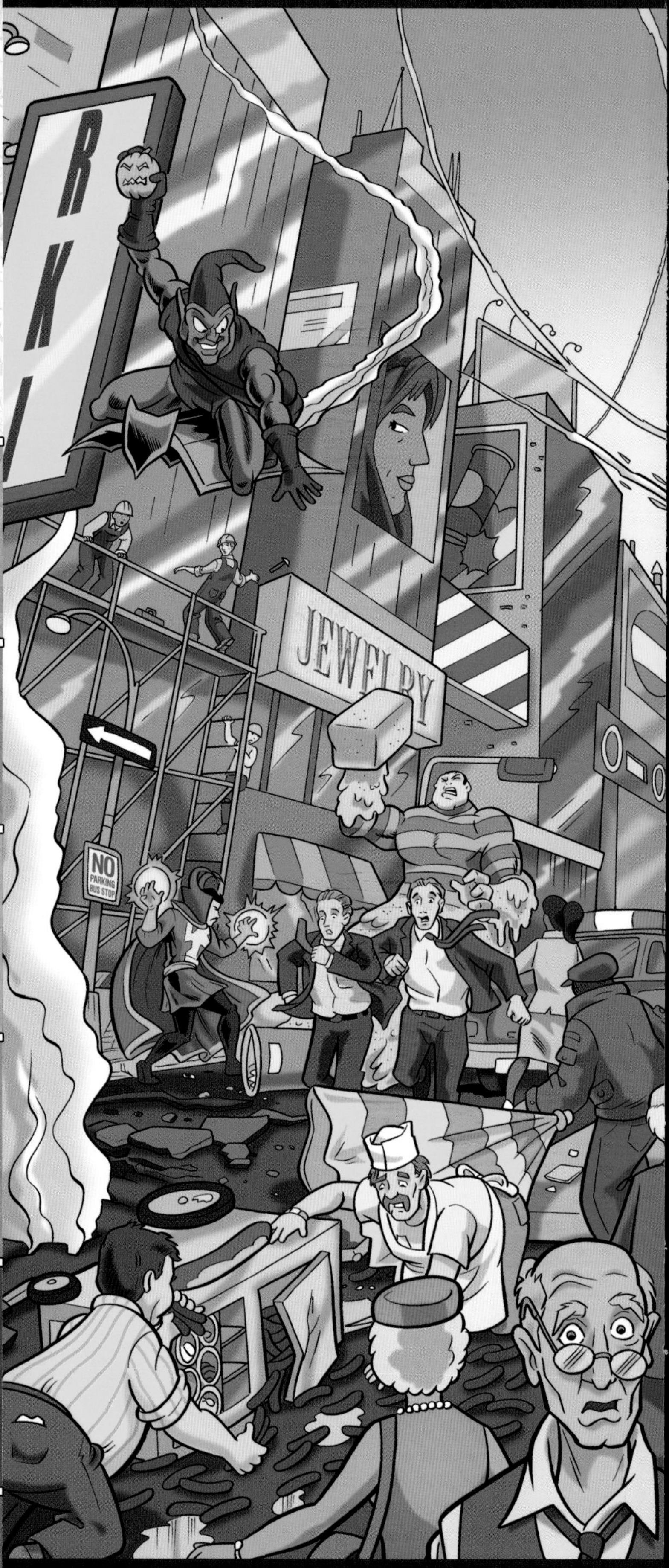
JEWELRY
NO PARKING BUS STOP

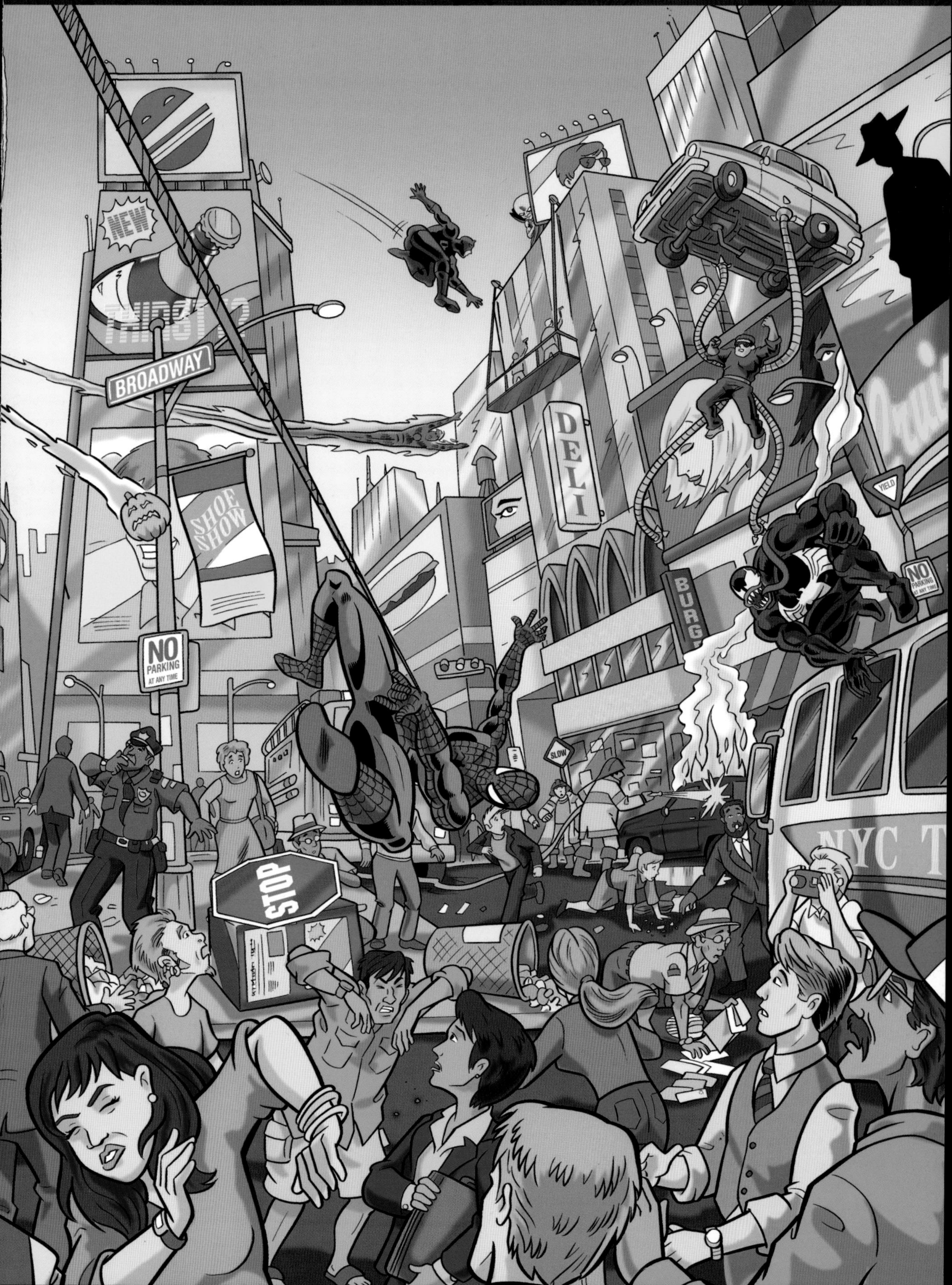
NEW
THIRSTY?
BROADWAY
SHOE SHOW
NO PARKING AT ANY TIME
DELI
STOP
SLOW
YIELD
NO PARKING AT ANY TIME

IF ROCKET AND GROOT WANT TO COME OUT AHEAD, THEY'LL HAVE TO GET INSIDE THE HEAD—OF KNOWHERE, THAT IS! COSMO, KNOWHERE'S HEAD OF SECURITY, ASSISTS THE DARING DUO DOWN INTO THE DANGEROUS MINES.

WHILE ROCKET USES GROOT AS A HANDY LADDER, LOOK FOR THESE SUBTERRANEAN TOOLS, INCLUDING 10 OF KNOWHERE'S BEST MINING PODS:

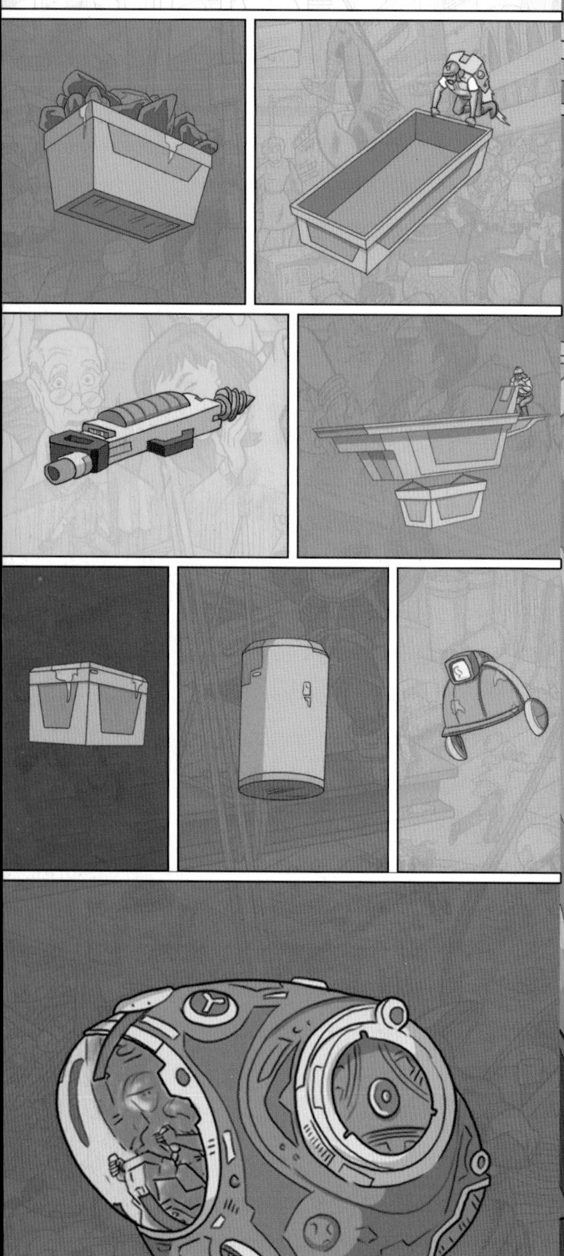

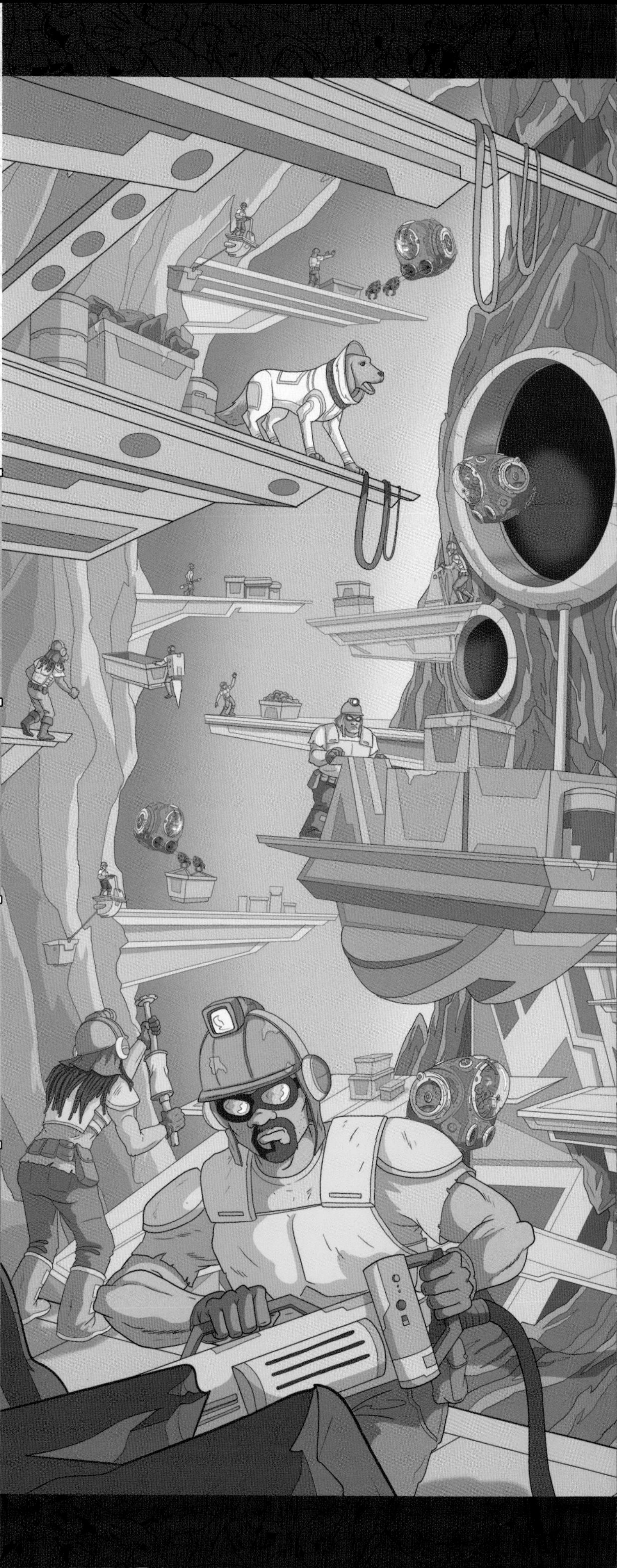

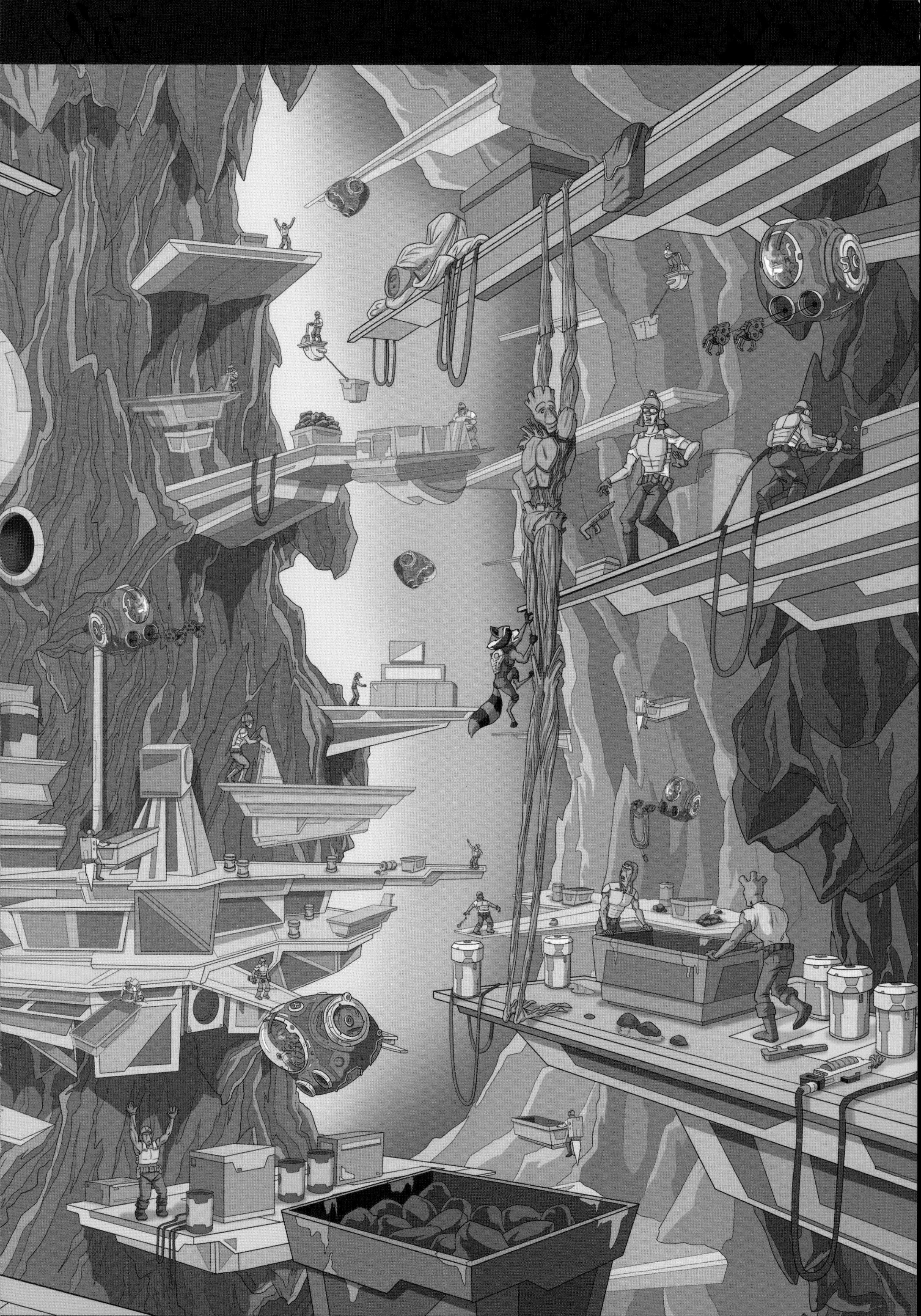

AFTER DEFEATING ALL OF HIS ENEMIES—WITH A LITTLE HELP FROM HIS FRIENDS—IRON MAN HAS ARRIVED BACK AT STARK INDUSTRIES. HE IS GREETED BY HIS MANY FANS, ALL HAPPY THAT HE'S SAVED THE PLANET FROM EVIL.

WHILE THE CROWD CHEERS ON OUR HERO, LOOK FOR IRON MAN ITEMS HIDDEN AROUND THE SCENE. A FEW OF IRON MAN'S FRIENDS HAVE ALSO TURNED OUT TO JOIN THE CELEBRATION! CAN YOU FIND THEM AMONG THE MULTITUDE?

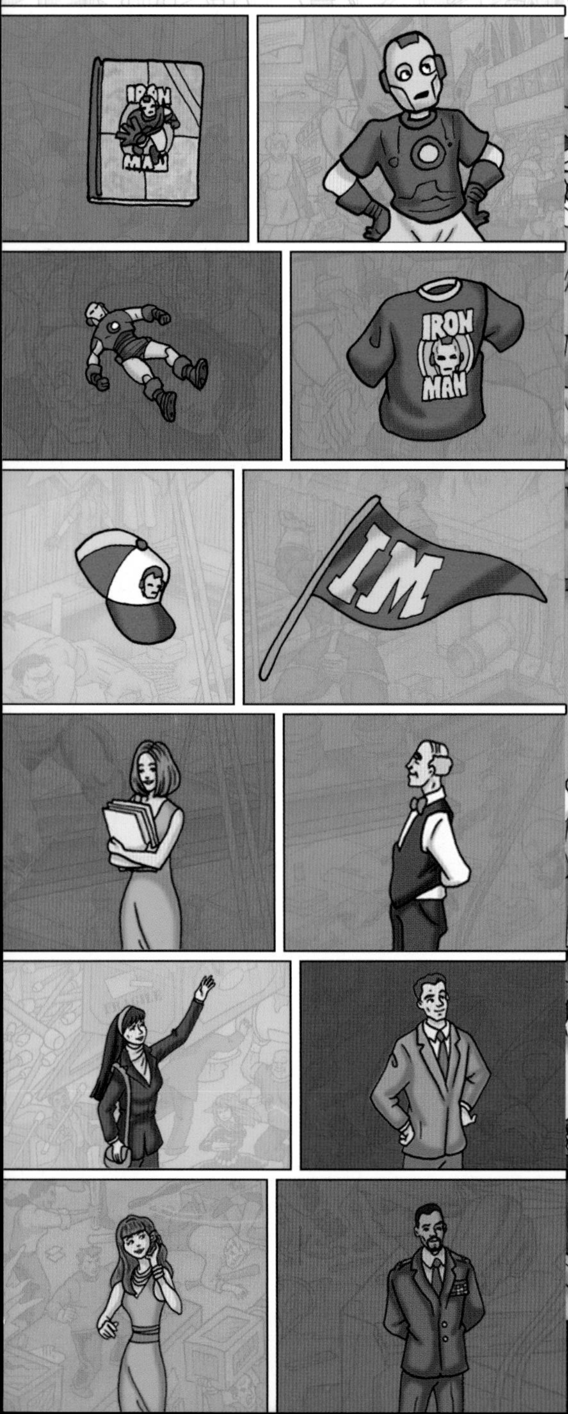

IRON MAN
IRON MAN
IM

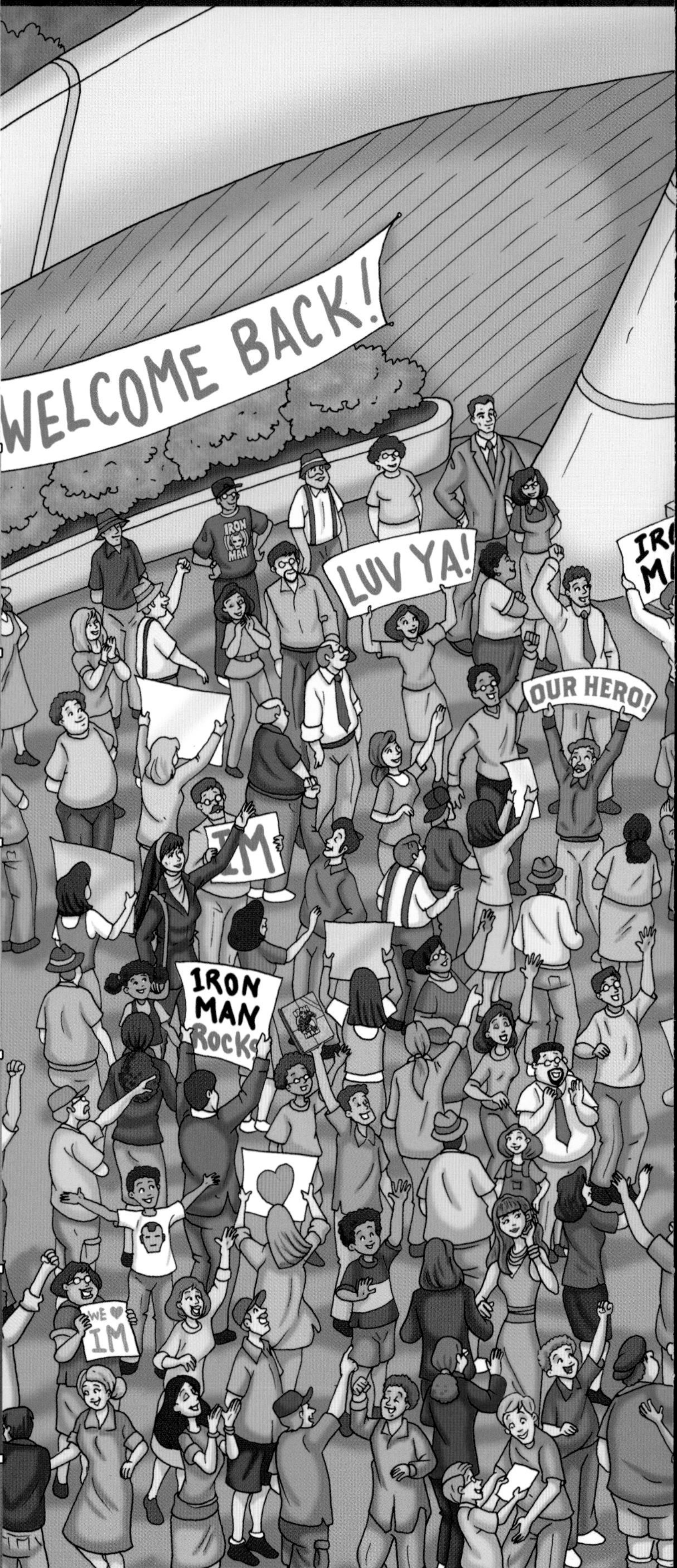

WELCOME BACK!
LUV YA!
OUR HERO!
IM
IRON MAN ROCKS
WE ♥ IM

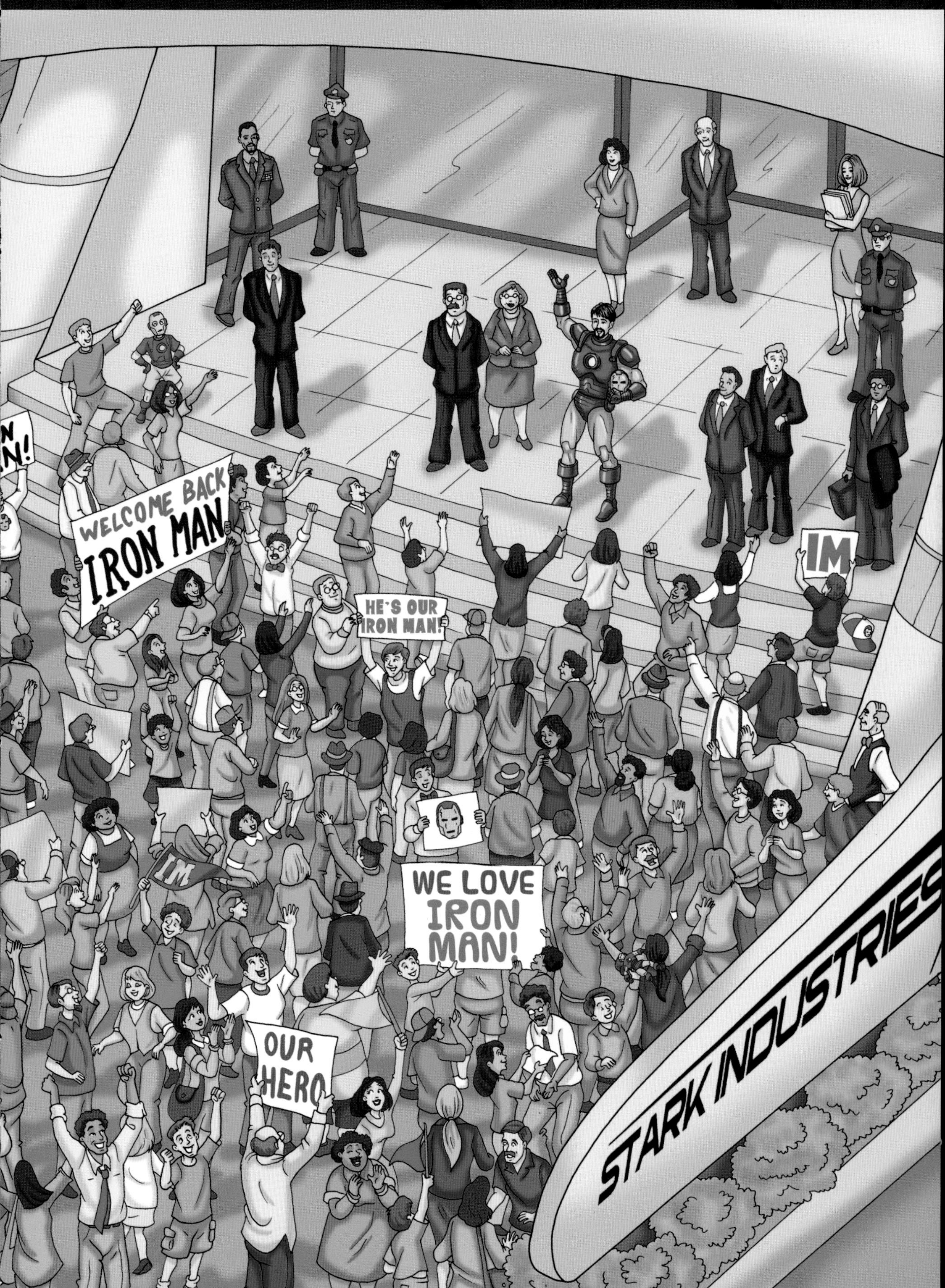
WELCOME BACK
IRON MAN
HE'S OUR
IRON MAN!
IM
IM
WE LOVE
IRON
MAN!
OUR
HERO
STARK INDUSTRIES

CROSSFIRE IS ATTEMPTING TO FLEE WITH STOLEN S.H.I.E.L.D. SECRETS! WHILE WASP GIVES CHASE, ANT-MAN TRANSFORMS INTO GIANT-MAN AND STOPS CROSSFIRE IN HIS TRACKS.

WE'VE REACHED THE END OF THIS TRIP! AS GIANT-MAN DELAYS THE FLIGHT, FASTEN YOUR SEATBELTS AND SCAN THE RUNWAY FOR THESE AIRCRAFT AND A FEW BEWILDERED BAGGAGE HANDLERS:

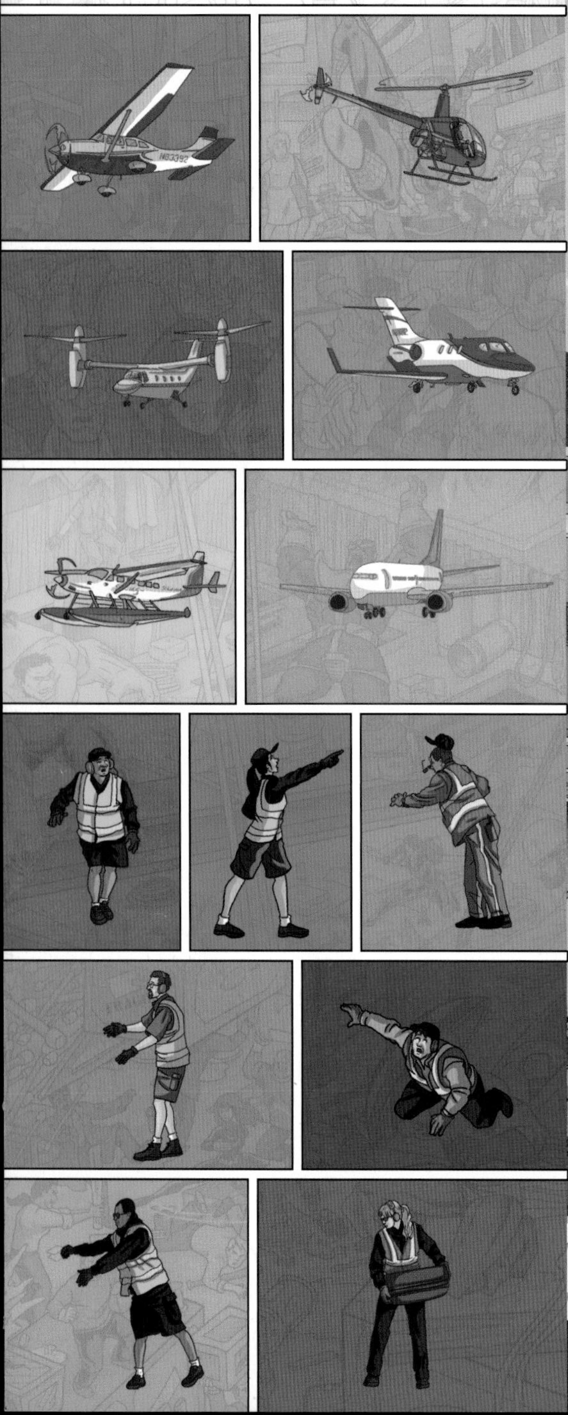
N83392

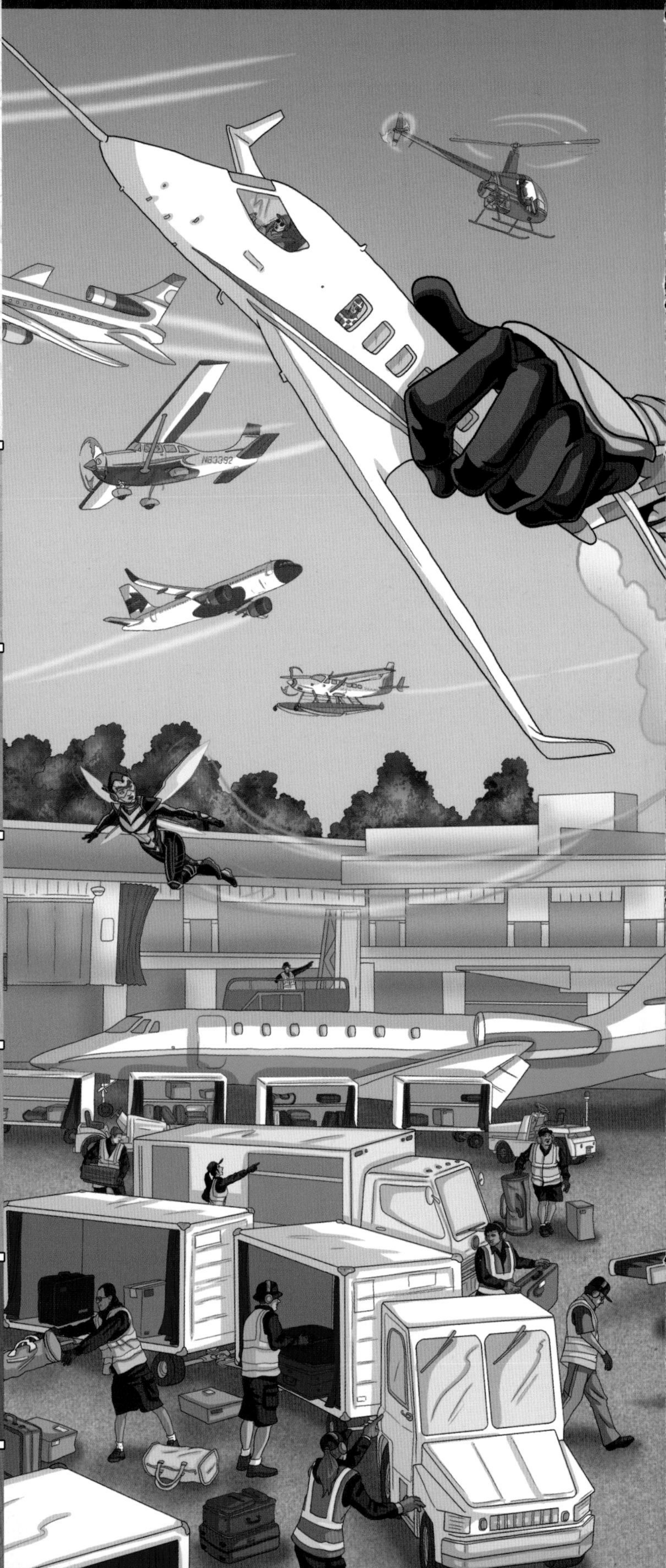
N83392

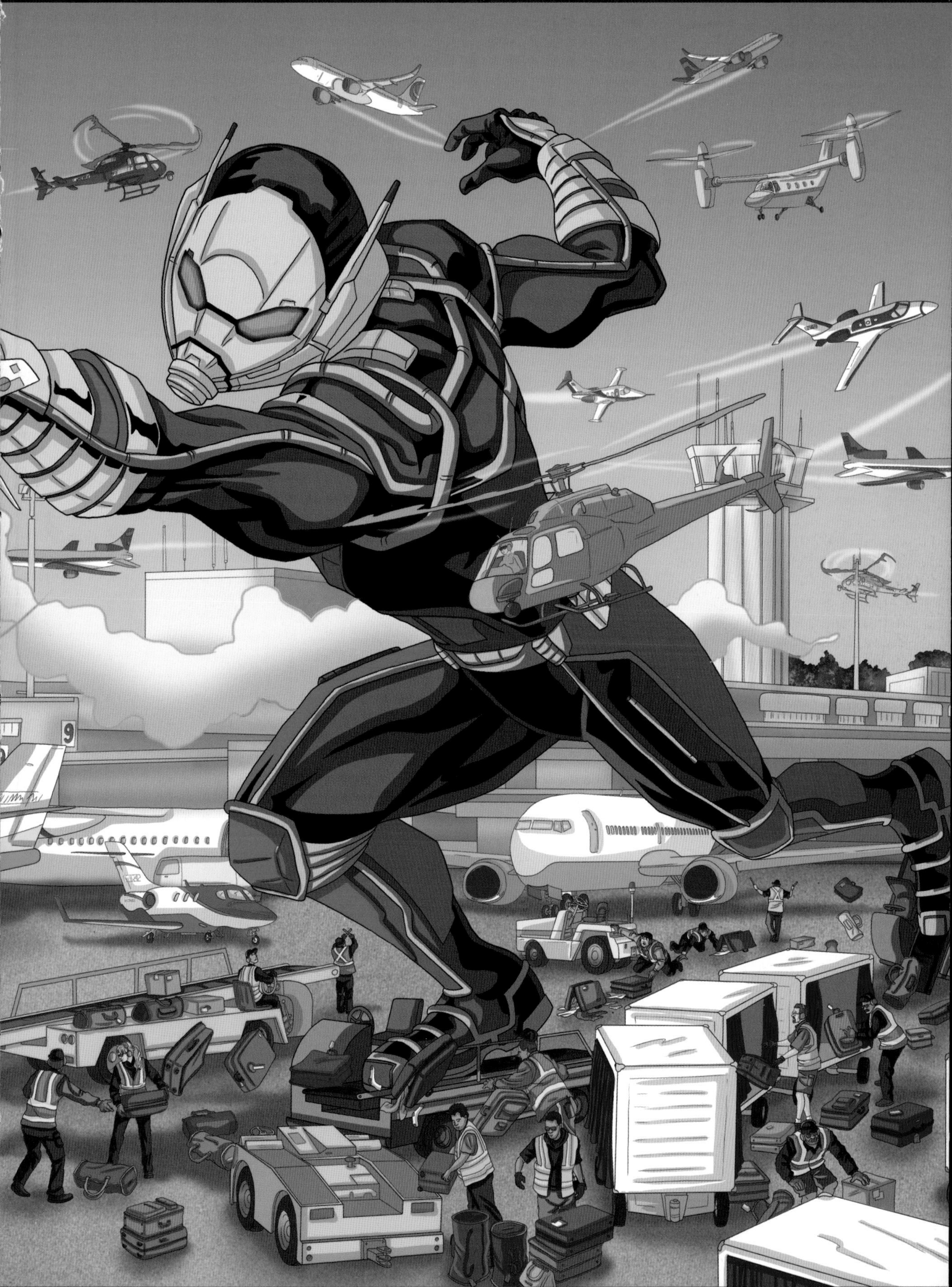
9

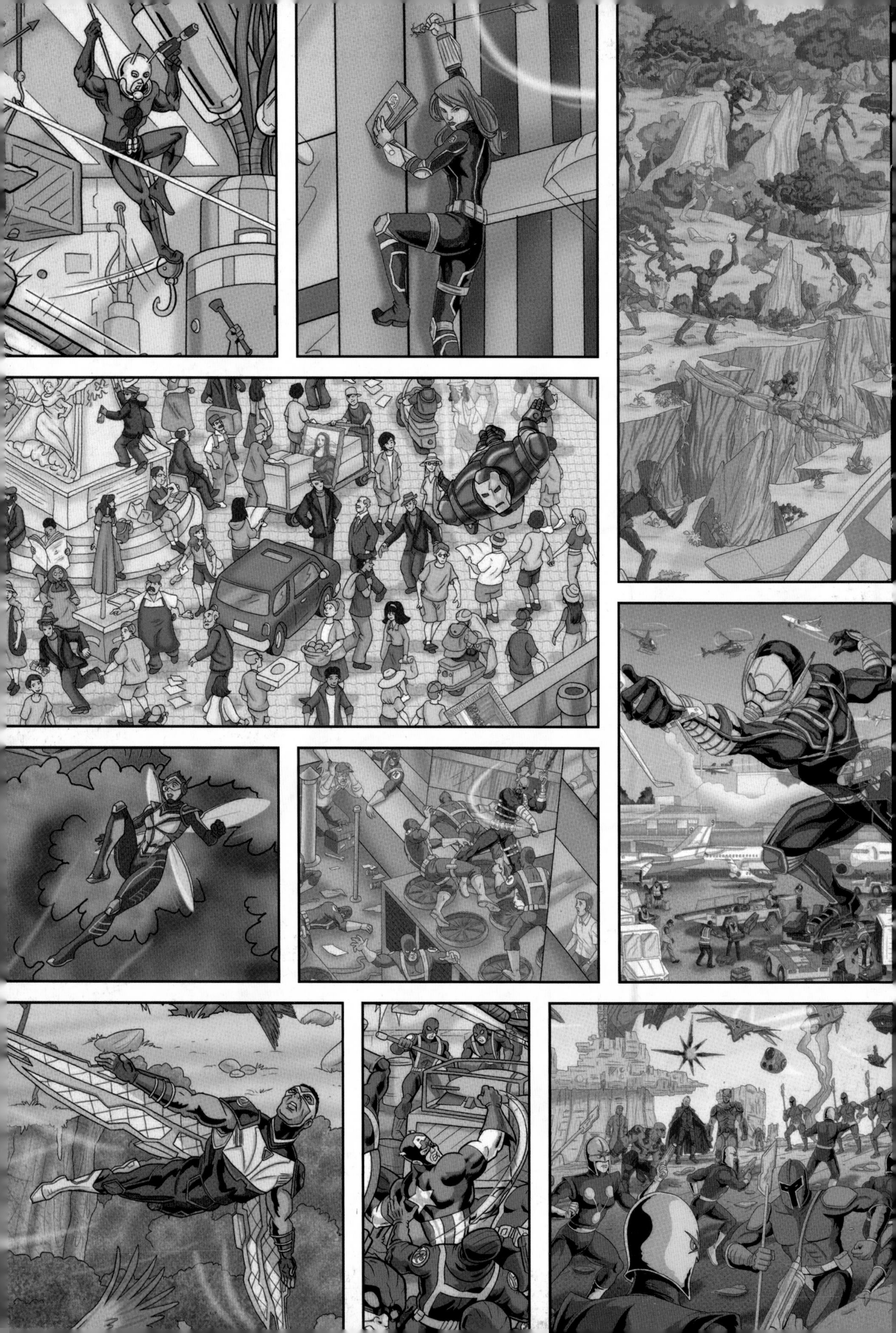